DARK FORTUNE

A lottery win changes everything for Kate: even her closest friend resents her luck. So, she starts a new life elsewhere, keeping her fortune a secret. However, it's soon apparent that someone who knows the truth is subjecting her to a campaign of fear. Kate doesn't know which of her new friends to trust. Could it be Dan, her attractive neighbour; Irene, who swiftly befriends her; or the more disturbing Fergal? Or could it be someone from her past?

SUSAN UDY

DARK FORTUNE

Complete and Unabridged

LINFORD
Leicester

First published in Great Britain in 2010

First Linford Edition
published 2012

British Library CIP Data

Udy, Susan.
    Dark fortune. - - (Linford romance library)
    1. Love stories.
    2. Large type books.
    I. Title II. Series
    823.9′14–dc23

    ISBN 978–1–4448–1326–5

Published by
F. A. Thorpe (Publishing)
Anstey, Leicestershire

Set by Words & Graphics Ltd.
Anstey, Leicestershire
Printed and bound in Great Britain by
T. J. International Ltd., Padstow, Cornwall

This book is printed on acid-free paper

Kate Moves To
The Country

Kate Brookes nervously twitched the bedroom curtain to one side and peered down through the darkness into her front garden. Her heart lurched. There was someone there; a man, she thought. Though, it was difficult to be sure, what with the top half of the figure being barely discernible, and in the shadow of the crab apple tree as it was.

It had been the squealing of the garden gate that had alerted her to the likelihood of someone being out there, that and the deep-throated growl of the dog lying on the floor beside her bed.

Without giving herself time to consider the possible danger that might be awaiting her outside, Kate left the safety of her bedroom and ran down the stairs, pulling on her dressing gown as she went. Jess followed, barking ferociously. Good, thought Kate, the more noise she made the better. Whoever was out there would know she had a dog with her, and so might think twice about loitering.

Stopping just long enough to grab a torch from the cupboard in the hallway, she held it in front of her, in the absence of any other weapon, and quietly turned the key in the front door.

'Stay close, Jess,' she whispered, totally unnecessarily, Jess was practically glued to the side of one of her legs, making walking a little tricky, but not impossible. Kate didn't care, however. Having the feel of the large dog so close more than made up for any awkwardness of movement. Nervous now, somewhat belatedly, she conceded, she inched the door open before thrusting the torch through the narrow gap and raking the garden with a beam of light.

'Who's there?'

No-one answered. Feeling fractionally braver, she opened the door wider. Again, she shone the light, but whoever had been out there had gone. The space beneath the crab apple tree was empty. They'd even closed the gate behind them, unless — No, she hadn't imagined the squealing of the gate or the figure standing so motionless. Someone had been there.

Knowing she'd be unable to sleep unless she checked that the intruder had indeed gone, she swiftly walked around the garden, shining the beam of the torch into every corner, around every bush. There was no-one there. The garden was deserted.

'There's no-one here, Jess.'

But Jess took no notice. She'd begun to sniff at the grass beneath the crab apple tree, right where the intruder had stood. Kate walked over and saw what she'd missed moments ago. A patch of grass had been flattened. Someone had definitely been there. Why? They'd made no move to enter the house, which, if they'd been intent on burglary, surely they would have? Why just stand there? Had whoever it was hoped she'd come out? If so, why had they disappeared before she had time to do so?

With a shiver, she swung and ran indoors. Whoever it had been could still be out there, beyond the garden somewhere, watching. It was then that she queried the wisdom of moving to such an isolated house. Maybe a suburban street would have been more sensible. With neighbours close enough to call on in times of trouble?

But the truth was, that after the events that had so unexpectedly overtaken her, and the sheer frenzy of it all, she'd been desperate for a place where no-one would know her. A place where she could keep herself to herself.

And her thoughts returned to that evening just a few weeks ago. It felt like years now.

It was Sally, her closest friend, who pushed her into buying a lottery ticket.

'It's a rollover week,' Sally declared. 'Eleven million pounds! Just think, Kate, if you win you could buy the Kwiksnak Cafe, instead of merely running it. And I could be your manager. On the other hand, if I win . . .'

'You know how I feel about the lottery,' Kate protested. 'You may as well tear up your money and throw it away. The end result's the same, the money's gone. Come on. What are the odds against winning? Millions to one? No thanks, I'd rather save any cash I've got and treat myself to a good holiday.'

Somehow though, Kate found herself paying a pound for a ticket; not five pounds or even ten pounds, just a pound. Chiefly, to try and shut Sally up.

'A pound's enough to lose,' Kate retaliated, not suspecting for a second how much wealth that pound was going to bring her.

In fact, her first instinct upon checking the numbers on the screen against her own numbers was to think she'd made a mistake. She checked them several more times before, in a complete dither, she rang Sally.

'Is this a joke?' Sally demanded. 'Because if it is . . . '

'No, no. I've got all the numbers!'

'You can't have — not with just a pound's worth!'

Sally sounded suspicious; outraged, even. Kate immediately felt guilty. Sally had been playing the lottery for years and hadn't won anything substantial.

'I have. What do I do? Sally?'

'Nothing. Don't do anything. I'm on my way round. You must have made a mistake.'

And that was the start of it.

There were times in the days afterwards when Kate wondered, if she'd known in advance what would happen, whether she would have left the money unclaimed? Because the truth was that everyone, even Sally, changed towards her. In fact, it was Sally who, despite being sworn to secrecy by Kate, blabbed to a friend, who then told another friend and so on.

It was the beginning of a nightmare. Of the phone calls, the begging letters. In the end, she simply stopped answering the phone, the door, and even opening the post. She literally hid away, cowering behind closed curtains; foolishly, because eventually, of course, she had to come out. There were things that she needed: food, for one; some fresh air, for another.

Finally, desperate to regain a semblance of normality, she returned to work. Only to realise almost at once that nothing would ever be the same again. Her life had been changed irrevocably and forever; a truth that was forcibly brought home to her when she overheard Sally complaining to one of the girls that they worked with.

'Don't you think all that money's changed her? I mean, I hardly see her — me, her best friend! Oh, she's trying to be friendly, but,' Sally sniffed. 'The times I rang her while she was at home, even called round and never got an answer. I suppose we aren't good enough for her any more. Well, she can keep her money. But when you think that it was me who persuaded her to buy the ticket, you'd expect her to . . . ' As if aware that Kate might be able to overhear, Sally's voice dropped to a whisper.

Even so, Kate could work out what she was saying; Sally thought she should share the money with her. Well, she needn't worry on that score. Kate fully intended to. She'd been merely waiting for the fuss to die away. But it wasn't only that. She genuinely hadn't wanted to speak to anyone, not even Sally. She couldn't quite forgive her for talking when she should have kept quiet. But even so, she'd never, not for a single second, considered keeping all that money to herself. But, nonetheless, that was the moment when Kate knew she couldn't go on like this.

Later that day, she told Sally, 'I fully intend to share my money with you.'

However, Sally refused to listen. 'You can keep your money, I don't want it.' Which had been a ridiculous thing to say when she quite clearly did.

Her friend's attitude proved the final straw for Kate. Spurred on by an almost overwhelming sense of injustice and misery, she decided to move, somewhere where people wouldn't know her. Where her private affairs would be just that: private. She even considered changing her name but then decided that was a bit too much. After all, the fuss would eventually die down.

It didn't take her long to find what she considered the perfect refuge, Bower Cottage, situated in a narrow lane, on the edge of a small village called Great Mindon. It was, she decided, a contradiction in terms. How could such a small village have acquired the name 'Great'?

She'd been given the details of the cottage by the first estate agent she visited and it proved to be love at first sight for Kate. With its thatched roof and half-timbered walls, its mullioned windows, its front door framed by a tangle of honeysuckle and roses, it was perfect.

Terrified of losing it, she offered the asking price and the cottage, already vacated by the owners, was hers. It wasn't until several days later that she'd asked herself, was it all a bit too quick? Maybe she should have given herself more time to consider every aspect of rural living? It was, after all, a far cry from the tower blocks of Birmingham, where she'd spent all of her life up till then.

But, whatever her doubts, the deed was done. She'd bought it. She had to go now.

* * *

'All right if we park here, luv?' one of the two removal men asked. They'd followed her in their van.

'It'll have to be,' Kate told them, climbing from her car. 'There's nowhere else.'

She'd occupied the only space available, in front of the garden gate. There was no driveway and no garage. Something she might think about trying to rectify when she'd been here for a while. The only thing the van driver could do was partially block the lane. Fortunately, there didn't seem to be a great deal of traffic needing to get past.

A hinge squealed as she opened the gate to lead the way along the weed strewn pathway to the front door. A branch of the gnarled crab apple tree that stood to one side brushed her head and a cluster of small orange fruits dropped off.

Kate looked around. She didn't remember the garden being this over-grown when she'd first viewed it. The grass was knee high and the honey-suckle and rose that sprawled across the front of the cottage were threatening to submerge it completely.

She had to push several tendrils to one side before unlocking the studded oak door and ushering the men inside with the first of the boxes.

By that evening, all of her furniture was in place and she'd unpacked most of her belongings. Hot and tired, and in desperate need of a break, she made herself a drink and a sandwich and took the makeshift meal into the back garden.

So far, she'd barely glanced through the kitchen window at it, but now, to her dismay, she saw that it was in an even worse state than the front, with overgrown roses, brambles, rampaging bindweed and nettles practically obliterating what must once have been charming flower beds and a lawn. The previous owners had left a wrought iron table and chairs on a minuscule patio, so at least she could sit down while she ate her meal and assessed the amount of work she needed to do to restore some sort of order. Mowing the grass and tidying the flower beds would be her first job.

'Hello-o? Anyone at home?'

'Oh, no!' Kate muttered. She'd

hoped for a few days, weeks even, of undisturbed peace. That was the reason she'd bought such an out of the way cottage, after all. She'd had more than enough of people and their blind prejudices.

Reluctantly, she put down her plate and walked back through the oak beamed sitting room to the front door. She was dismayed to see it wide open, and even more dismayed to see a man striding across the room towards her.

A Neighbour Calls

With the light behind him from the still open door, Kate found it impossible to distinguish the man's features. That made her nervous enough. Had she been found out already? Was he here to demand money with menaces? Don't be silly, she told herself. He'd hardly have announced his arrival if that was the case.

'Hi,' he said, 'no need to look so alarmed. I let myself in, your door was unlocked.' With that, he thrust out a hand. 'Dan Peters, your one, or I should say, your only neighbour.' He grinned and raised his other hand. It held a bottle of champagne. 'Sorry, did I frighten you?'

'No, no,' she lied, proffering her own hand. 'Kate, Kate Brookes.' She relaxed. 'It's-um, it's good of you to call.' Bit of a cheek though, she couldn't help thinking, to just walk in. But maybe that was the way they did things round here? If it was, she'd have to get used to it. Although, she'd have thought, as it was his first visit and she was a complete stranger, good manners would have dictated that he knock.

She stood to one side and allowed him to pass her before she went and pointedly closed the door. Still slightly apprehensive, she turned back to him. Neighbour or not, one couldn't be too careful nowadays.

However, he wasn't much bigger than she was, just a couple of inches taller than her five feet six; he was also lightly built, and attractive. A mop of fair hair flopped down onto his forehead, beneath which bright blue eyes glinted; his mouth beamed with what looked like utter delight. She felt like first prize in a raffle. His delight seemed rather excessive for an initial meeting.

He merely stood, clearly expecting her to take the lead. Kate did just that and headed for the kitchen. She sensed rather than saw the manner in which his glance travelled over her.

'I'm sitting in the garden,' she told him, 'trying to work out how long it will take me to restore some sort of order to what has, frankly, been transformed into a jungle since I last saw it.'

He waved the bottle again. 'If you've got some glasses handy, we could take this out with us and discuss it together. I'm a keen gardener and rather pride myself on what I consider my green fingers. I could help.'

Kate hadn't as yet found the crystal flutes that had originally belonged to her parents, who had since passed away, but she had uncovered some plain wine glasses. She pulled them from the cupboard. 'Will these do?'

'They most certainly will.' He uncorked the champagne with a dramatic flourish after which he had to hurriedly fill the glasses that Kate held out to prevent the frothing liquid from spilling out of the bottle. 'To your health and happiness. It's good to meet you, Kate Brookes.'

He followed Kate into the garden. 'Aah,' he exclaimed, looking around. 'I see what you mean. Still, shouldn't take too long to tame it.' His glance swept back to Kate once more, his expression now one of pure speculation. 'So, you're going to be living here alone then?'

'My word,' Kate murmured, 'the village drums have been busy.'

Dan didn't look in any way put out by this. In fact, he seemed amused. The blue eyes danced as he said, 'You'll have to get used to everybody knowing your business, I'm afraid. We're a very close community here. Um, where did you say you come from?'

'I didn't say, but it's Birmingham.'

'Aah, yes.'

'You know it?'

'Not very well. I've had to go there occasionally on business. No time for any sightseeing.' His gaze narrowed. 'So, tell me, what made you leave the bright lights of a city and come here? To the opposite end of the spectrum, so to speak?'

17

'I wanted a quieter life.' If the other villagers were as inquisitive as this man, she was going to have her work cut out to keep her secret. She'd never been any good at lying, her voice would tremble, her cheeks redden — they always gave her away.

'Well, you'll get that here all right. Only trouble is, it could be a bit too quiet. Not much goes on.' He continued to study her through half-closed eyes. Kate began to feel uncomfortable. He was suspicious. After all the trouble she'd gone to to remain incognito. Instead, all he said was, 'Your friends will miss you.'

She smiled coolly. 'For a while, maybe; they'll soon get over it.'

'Will we be seeing any of them?' He slowly sipped his champagne, still watching over the rim of his glass.

'I wouldn't think so. Why don't you tell me a bit about yourself?' She decided it was safer to change the subject. He'd been about to ask her why she didn't expect her friends to visit her and, let's face it, what could she say? *'Well, they're all so jealous of my good fortune that they no longer want anything to do with me.'* She didn't think so. She had no intention of broadcasting her newly acquired prosperity. That would surely defeat the object of her coming here.

Luckily, and just as she'd gambled he would, he seemed more than willing to talk about himself. But then, mused Kate, weren't most people?

'Well, I'm divorced,' he pulled a wry face. 'Have you been married? Or maybe you still are?' His gaze went to her empty ring finger.

'No, 'fraid not.'

'Oh, I shouldn't be afraid, it doesn't always work out.' His expression darkened. 'And, sadly, as well as losing a wife, I lost a job. All within a month of each other. I know,' he gave a bitter little laugh, 'careless, you might say.'

'No,' Kate diplomatically murmured, wondering why any sane woman would leave such an attractive and likeable man?

'Not all my fault,' he went on. 'The job went through redundancy. The top brass reckoned they needed to save money, to downsize, so ... ' he shrugged, 'that meant dispensing with me. However, on a lighter note, I'm a committed member of our little community, I play golf regularly. I'm an only child. My parents retired to Spain a few years ago now. Anything else you'd like to know?'

Kate stiffened. There was something in his look as he said that; something not immediately identifiable. Defiance, maybe? Was he expecting her to judge him? Given her own circumstances, that was the last thing she was likely to do. 'I'm, I'm sorry. I didn't mean to pry.' Good heavens. Why was she apologising? He'd started the interrogation.

He must have sensed her exasperation, because he quickly said, 'No need to apologise. I'm happy for you to know all about me. I've no secrets.'

Kate's heart lurched once again. He

might not have recognised her but he could have sensed she was keeping things back. It would explain the looks he'd given her.

'So, tell me, what did you do in Birmingham?'

When his voice betrayed no hint of censure, Kate decided she was imagining things. He was just interested in her. Maybe liked her. All right, so he was a tad nosy, but there was no harm in telling him a little about herself, was there? It needn't be a disaster. She'd just have to know what to leave out. And let's face it, if life here was as uneventful as he had said, she couldn't blame him for asking questions. A new face must be a cause for celebration.

She'd have to try and not be so sensitive. That had always been a problem for her. Even as a child. Her mother had frequently been forced to say, 'Kate, darling, you'll have to grow a thicker skin. Yours is much too thin.'

She never had, though. Which is possibly why she'd reacted so badly to her friends' behaviour in the aftermath of her lottery win. She really had to start to behave in a more adult fashion. Learn to parry intrusive questions, bend the truth a little. And she'd start right now. 'I was a manageress of a cafe.' She deliberately kept it vague.

'You made redundant too?'

'Well, s-something l-like that.' Just listen to her — stuttering and stammering. What had happened to her newfound resolution? He was going to see straight through her.

'Oh, come on, you can tell me,' he gently encouraged. 'We're in the same boat. There's nothing to be ashamed of.'

'I'm not ashamed. It's just that there's nothing to tell. I simply wanted a change.' The words came out more sharply than she had intended, solely as a result of her edginess at having to practice such deception.

He looked startled; hurt. The increasingly familiar sense of misery suffused her. How was she ever going to make friends when she couldn't tell people the truth about herself? When she had to watch everything she said? Maybe she should come clean? But if she did that, she risked the same sort of things that had happened in Birmingham happening here. And she wouldn't be able to bear it. And then, what if people sought her out simply because of her wealth? She wanted to be liked for herself. Was that too much to ask for?

'Do you have any family?' Her sharpness clearly hadn't inhibited Dan's interest in her.

'No, not any more.' Kate made a concerted effort to speak normally. After all, he was just being neighbourly — something which, at one time, she wouldn't have given a second thought to. 'My father died in a car accident seven years ago and my mother died eighteen months later. I don't have any siblings.'

'You must have been very young.'

'Twenty, when my mother died.'

'How did you manage alone?'

He looked genuinely concerned. It

made Kate feel even worse about her deception.

'I-I sold the family house, which was too much of a responsibility for me at that time, and moved into a flat. Got myself a job.'

'No university then?'

'No. I'd been to catering college, so I went to work as assistant cook at the cafe and worked my way up from there to manageress.'

'Not bad for, what, a twenty-five — twenty six year old?' He tilted his head to one side and subjected her to an intent scrutiny. 'Am I right?'

'More or less. No, I suppose it wasn't bad.'

'And you've left that to come here. What do you plan to do now? Get a job? Or are you a woman of means these days?'

Kate glanced at him, carefully schooling her expression into one of impassivity. Besides having a skin so thin it was almost transparent, and being totally incapable of uttering a falsehood that was in any way convincing, her face, too, had always been something of an open book. It had been her undoing many a time in the wake of a misdeed. Her mother would sigh, 'Oh, Kate.' It had seemed easiest to simply confess then.

'Well, you must have made a good deal of money on the sale of your parents' house. Sorry.' He'd clearly sensed her discomfort and annoyance at his probing. 'Put my interest down to having lived in a small village for several years and being the butt of local nosiness for almost as long. It's led me to believe it's a God-given right to ask questions and, moreover, to expect answers.'

He gave a short laugh. 'You'll have to forgive me and, I suspect, the major proportion of the local community, because they'll all want to know all about you. There aren't many secrets in this village.' He gave a chuckle, unaware of the stab of panic that his light words induced within Kate. 'So, if you've any skeletons in the cupboard, best to pull them out straight away and dispose of them.'

Kate's heart sank. Again, she considered telling the truth before she was discovered to be a liar. But something stopped her. So all she said was, 'You're right, I did make some money, but I've invested most of it for the future.'

She saw him glance at the cottage behind them.

'I did use some of it, obviously, to buy Bower Cottage.' And that's all I'm telling you, she mutely added, for now, at any rate. Maybe, once she'd got to know people, she'd feel able to confide her good fortune. But, just at the moment, she had no intention of revealing that without her lottery win she'd never have been able to afford such a lovely cottage. She hadn't made nearly enough on the sale of the family home. It had been difficult enough just to sell it. She'd had to drop the price twice.

'Well, I must go.' He drained his glass. 'Lots to do. Once again, welcome to Great Mindon. I hope you'll be happy here. I drink in the village pub, the Red Lion, most evenings, along with many of the locals, so if you feel like coming along, I'll introduce you to everyone. I'm sure they'll take you to their hearts — just like I've done,' and, with a grin, he left her to make what she would of that last tantalising remark.

Kate Gets Out
And About

Just as she'd feared it would, the loneliness of Kate's situation very swiftly began to manifest itself, driving her to take Dan up on his invitation to join him at the Red Lion pub. Despite her initial alarm when he'd walked uninvited into the cottage, and then her unease at his shameless probing, by the time he'd left she'd found herself well on the way to liking him.

So much so, that she was disappointed to discover he wasn't there. When she asked the man behind the bar about him, he told her, 'I haven't seen him for a night or two. Maybe he's gone to see that lad of his in Wales.'

'Lad of his?' Kate asked.

'Yes, his son, Nicky. He lives there with his mother and her new husband.'

He'd looked curiously at Kate then. 'You didn't know?'

'No, he didn't mention a son.' Kate wondered why not? He'd been open about practically everything else about himself and his lifestyle. Had he thought such knowledge would put her off getting to know him better?

'Are you the new owner of Bower Cottage by any chance?'

'Yes.'

'Dan told me you'd moved in and he'd called. He said you might be visiting one evening.' He held out a hand. 'Jack Worth, landlord of this place. Pleased to meet you.'

Kate took the proffered hand. 'Kate Brookes.'

'Right, what can I get you to drink then? It's on the house.'

As Kate walked back home some time later, she made a point of slowing down as she passed Dan's house. There wasn't a light to be seen. Maybe Jack Worth was right and he was away? She wondered when he'd planned to tell her he had a son. The omission made her feel a little less guilty about her own lack of honesty.

A couple of mornings later, she decided she'd walk into the village and explore. The workmen had arrived to start the alterations that she had decided to have done and she sensed that they'd rather be left alone to get on. She'd decided to leave the sitting room as it was; with its low, beamed ceiling and inglenook fireplace, it needed no further embellishment, and the dining room only wanted a coat of fresh paint, which she was going to tackle herself.

It didn't take Kate as long as she'd expected to walk to the village, but even if it had taken an hour or two, it would have been well worth it. The day was a gloriously sunny one, the summer sky the depth of blue that one only expected to see in hotter climes; the hedgerows were full of dog roses and aromatic, wild honeysuckle, its blossom bedecked tendrils home, by the sound of it, to a million bees.

Once she reached Great Mindon, she found, as she'd known she would from her initial viewing of the cottage and its neighbourhood, a butcher, a grocer and greengrocer, a newsagent-cum-post office, and the pub, of course; there was even a second-hand book shop nestling in between a gentlemen's outfitters and a small cafe. In the midst of all of this, a church and its adjoining hall sat. She made the newsagent her first port of call. She'd buy the local paper, that was always a good source of news and information.

'Good morning.' The smiling post-mistress walked out from behind her protective glass screen to stand behind a counter that displayed an unexpectedly comprehensive selection of magazines and newspapers. 'You must be Kate Brookes.'

Did everyone know who she was, Kate mused. Fortunately, no-one seemed to have connected her to the lottery winner of the same name. Or maybe they just didn't read the papers? 'Yes, that's right.'

'I'm Betty Forman. My husband and I run this place, although he's out at the moment. Oh, hello, Irene.' She peered around Kate. ''You're just in time to meet our newest resident, Kate Brookes. Kate, this is Irene Willoughby, and with her is Jess.'

Kate swung to see a slender, silver-haired woman standing behind her, at her side was a beautiful golden retriever. 'Irene's lived here all her life so you couldn't find anyone more fitted to tell you about Great Mindon and its inhabitants.'

'Tssk.' Irene clicked her tongue, half in annoyance and half in amusement. 'That makes me sound like the village busybody, Betty.'

'Oh no, I didn't mean ... ' Betty Forman looked anxiously at the older woman, 'Oh, dear.'

'It's all right, I know what you meant.' And Irene gave a broad smile, at the same time shaking Kate's hand.

She glanced down at the dog. It sat

patiently, its liquid brown eyes fixed intently upon her. Kate bent down and stroked its silken head. The dog responded by pushing its wet nose into her palm and wagging its tail with great energy and enthusiasm. She looked back up at Irene. 'I've been thinking I might get myself a dog — it would be someone to walk with.' Now where on earth had that idea come from? She'd never owned as much as a hamster before.

However, if Kate was astonished by what she'd just said, Irene didn't seem at all surprised. In fact, she smiled, the skin at the corners of her pale blue eyes crinkling. 'If you're serious about that, I could maybe help you out. I'm looking for a new home for Jess.' The smile disappeared and the wrinkles around her eyes deepened. She suddenly looked much older than the sixty-five or so years that Kate had guessed at.

'Irene!' Betty was visibly shocked. 'This is the first I've heard of this. Are you sure? You love that dog. You've never been without one.'

'I know, and no, I'm not really sure Although I'm still reasonably fit for seventy-eight,' Kate was every bit as shocked as the postmistress. She'd never have had Irene down as that old, 'I'm simply not fit enough for the length of walk she needs each day. And what with my arthritis playing up like it is — some mornings I can hardly get out of bed, let alone cover the miles she demands: It's not fair on Jess — is it, girl?' She bent and tenderly patted the dog's head. Jess wagged her tail and woofed back at her.

'Well, if you mean it?' Kate didn't know what to say. She hadn't anticipated such a response. She hoped Irene didn't think she'd been dropping hints.

But Irene's next words firmly disabused her of that notion. 'Oh, I mean it,' Irene frowned, 'or, at least, I think I do. She's obviously taken a fancy to you, otherwise I never would have mentioned it. Look, I tell you what, why don't you come round to my place and start taking her for a few walks? You and

I will get to know each other and it will get Jess used to you. See if you get on together, although I'm guessing you will if first reactions are anything to go by. I wouldn't want her to go to anyone who wasn't going to love her as much as I do.' The anguish at the mere notion of having to part with her pet was written clearly upon her face, within her eyes.

'Oh no, of course you wouldn't,' Kate hastened to agree. No danger of that, she reflected, she was already in love with the gentle-looking animal. The inky eyes stared up at her. 'I think that sounds a wonderful idea. So, how about tomorrow? About this time.'

'Right. That's agreed then.'

★　★　★

The following morning, Kate walked to Irene's cottage situated halfway along the village high street, the middle one of a small terrace of three, where Irene greeted her with the degree of enthusiasm and warmth she would have only expected after knowing someone for years instead of a mere day.

It was starting to look as if it wasn't only Jess who'd taken to her. The suspicion cheered Kate. For she'd taken to Irene as well, despite the vast difference in their ages.

'Come in and have a cup of coffee before you set off. You'll need the caffeine. I'll warn you now, she'll walk you miles, so I hope you're wearing suitable shoes.' She glanced down at Kate's sensible footwear and beamed her approval.

'I don't care. I love walking. I always regretted that I didn't have the opportunity, or time, when I lived in Birmingham,' Kate replied, bending down to the dog who'd come bounding into the kitchen and, just as she had the day before, pressed her nose into Kate's waiting hand, tail working like a piston. The growing rapport between the animal and herself banished Kate's last few doubts about her suitability for taking care of the lovely animal. 'But I will have that dose of caffeine first. Then, we ought to discuss the matter of payment if Jess and I do decide we like each other, although, for my part, I've got no doubts. She's gorgeous, aren't you, girl?' The dog gave a soft bark. It was, for all the world, as if she were agreeing with Kate.

'Payment? For Jess?' Irene looked shocked. 'Oh no, I don't want anything. I just want her to go to a good home; to someone who will love her as I do.' Her voice broke. 'Oh dear, will you look at me? Sentimental old fool that I am.' Visibly exasperated with herself for her show of emotion, she dashed the tears away.

Kate felt terrible. As much as she wanted Jess, she wondered if she was being selfish? She was, after all, planning to deprive this old lady of her sole companion. 'Look, I've been thinking.' The answer to both their needs had just occurred to her. 'Why don't you keep her and I'll just come and walk her? That way you could manage and I'd get the exercise.'

'Oh no, dear, that wouldn't be at all fair to you or Jess. And you need a dog where you're living, both for company and protection. Although,' she glanced fondly down at the dog, 'how much protection Jess would prove to be, I don't really know. She'd probably lick an intruder to death, rather than attack him.

'She's never been put to the test — fortunately for me. Anyway,' she briskly went on, 'you don't need to worry about me. I'll get a cat. That way, I'll have the company without the trouble of exercising it. No, Jess deserves a younger owner. I should never have had her, I've known that for quite some time — ever since this arthritis got worse. Mind you, she's always been a bit too exuberant for me.'

'Are you absolutely sure?' Kate couldn't shake off the feeling of guilt.

'Yes, positively. Of course, I wouldn't object if you both call and see me on a regular basis.' Her voice broke once more, but, just as before, she made a swift recovery. She was clearly determined that nothing should stand in the way of Kate having Jess, certainly not her own wavering emotions. 'Now, cream and sugar, is it? And I want to hear all about you and how you came to move to Great Mindon.'

★   ★   ★

Kate breathed deeply. This was wonderful after the fume-laden air of Birmingham. It had been Irene who had told her about the walk by the river.

'You can let Jess off the lead there, she likes that. You'll just have to watch she doesn't try and keep up with the ducks. She's got so carried away once or twice, she's ended up in the river with them,' she'd chuckled fondly. 'Which, with the bank being so steep, caused something of a problem when it came to getting back out again.'

Kate looked down at the ducks now, paddling along beneath them, keeping pace with her as she threw the pieces of bread that Irene had given her. Jess was striding ahead watching the quacking birds. She obviously had no intention of accidentally joining them in their swim today.

How could she ever have had doubts about coming here? It was perfect and with Jess as her companion it would be positively idyllic. There'd been one sticky moment when Irene had demanded to know what had made her move to the village. Kate had said the same thing that she'd said to Dan, that she was hankering after a quieter life.

If they ever got round to comparing notes, they would, at least, both tell the same story. She still felt bad about lying, particularly to Irene whom she fervently hoped would become a friend, but she really couldn't see any other way. Despite the fact that her fears of people's nosiness didn't seem to be about to materialise. Except for Dan, initially that is, and she hadn't seen anything more of him since that first visit. Although, he must have returned from wherever he'd been because she'd noticed some windows open when she'd walked by his house that morning.

She glanced up from the ducks to check on where Jess was — she didn't want to lose her; that would be a disaster on their first walk together — and saw someone approaching along the footpath. It was a man. He was tall — six feet one or two, she estimated. He too was walking a dog. He also was the first person she'd seen. That was what had struck her, the fact that there was no-one else around. If she'd been doing this in Birmingham, she'd have been just one amongst many.

However, it was that very solitude that now induced a pang of misgiving. Don't be silly, she chided herself. This wasn't a crime-ridden city. This was Great Mindon. In an effort to reassure herself as much as to be pleasant, she smiled at him as he got closer.

He didn't respond. Instead, his

glance measured her, coolly, impassively.

'Good morning,' he eventually said, mainly, she suspected, because he had to stop to allow her to pass him on the narrow path. His dog immediately ran to Jess and, with a whimper, began to sniff at her. 'Sam,' he said, 'come here.' He still didn't smile. 'Um — isn't that Irene Willoughby's dog?' He spoke curtly, almost censoriously.

'Yes. I'm walking her for Irene,' Kate told him. Although what business it was of his she couldn't imagine.

'I see. Always best to ask, don't you think?'

Kate, declined to answer that. What had he thought she was doing, for goodness sake? Making off with Jess? Did she look like a dog thief?

'I'm Fergal Cameron. I live at The Old Hall.'

He held out a hand. Kate took it. 'I'm Kate Brookes. I've just moved into Bower Cottage.'

'A-ah, yes, I heard.'

'You and everyone else,' she muttered.

A glint of what looked suspiciously like amusement flashed into his face, despatching the expression of censure and tilting his mouth slightly at one corner. However, as it was gone almost as quickly as it had appeared and his expression had reverted to just the right side of frigid, Kate decided she'd imagined it.

'You're organising the protest against the new road, aren't you?' It was Irene who'd told her about the dual carriageway to be built between nearby Oxbridge and Worcester. It would virtually run across one end of the village, destroying its tranquillity forever.

It would also swallow up a substantial slice of Fergal Cameron's garden. 'Not that he'll miss it that much,' Irene had said. 'He'll still have about four acres to play with. Still, I can see his point. Who wants a dual carriageway next door? But the real danger is to Box Wood.'

43

This was a piece of woodland half a mile or so outside of Great Mindon. 'They'll have to fell that completely, and it's home to an enormous variety of wildlife. It's nothing short of criminal. We've tried all sorts to stop it, petitions, letters to the local paper, the council — we even contacted BBC News. They did do a feature on it in Midlands Today, but no-one takes a scrap of notice. So, it's going ahead. So frustrating. People's feelings don't seem to matter any more,' he said.

'It won't directly affect you, I know, as you're on the other side of the village, but we could use all the help we can get for our protest. They're planning to start felling Box Wood next week and we were hoping for a sizeable demonstration, you know, tying ourselves together and to trees, that sort of thing. To stop the bulldozers and chain saws. Are you up for it?' Fergal looked at her.

No! She certainly wasn't. The mere notion of lying in the path of a bulldozer was enough to turn Kate's blood cold, let alone actually doing it. She'd never been confrontational, much preferring to avoid trouble of any sort. If she possibly could. And, as he'd pointed out, it wouldn't affect her; her cottage was a safe distance away.

'Well, it isn't really my sort of thing . . . ' She limped into silence.

'I see.' His words were even more clipped and terse, and she wouldn't have deemed that possible. But it was his expression that really conveyed his sentiments about her feeble excuse. If it had been cool before, Kate deemed it capable now of freezing the river that flowed so freely by. It was enough to spur her into blurting, 'Oh, why not? Count me in.'

It might not be going to affect her directly, as he'd pointed out, but she did live in the village, so she supposed she ought to do her bit to preserve it and its immediate surroundings. And she could always make sure that she kept well away from the front line.

'Good!'

At last, a genuine smile. It transformed the severe planes of his face into something that was positively handsome. It would be worth placing herself beneath the treads of the fearsome bulldozer just to see it a second time!

'I'm holding a meeting this evening in the church hall so that we can organise things. Can you attend?'

'Yes, no problem. I only have myself to consider.'

'So I've heard.'

'Right — well, I'll be on my way.' Kate smiled weakly up at him and made to pass him and continue her walk. She was already regretting her agreement to take part in his demonstration. Whatever had possessed her? For years now, she'd taken care to steer well clear of good-looking men — ever since she'd had her heart seriously broken by one.

The Village Is United

Despite repeatedly telling herself she wouldn't go to the meeting, that no-one would miss her presence, due to the fact that she knew hardly anyone yet, on the dot of seven o'clock that evening, Kate found herself walking into the church hall. To her astonishment, the place was crammed full; she wouldn't have thought the village boasted this many people.

With all the seats taken, they'd been forced to resort to standing around the edges of the room; to the extent that they were even spilling out of the door. Despite that, it only took her a second to pick out Irene. She'd managed to bag herself a seat in the front row. Kate smiled to herself. She should have known she would. There was a lot of the matriarch of the village about Irene. The old lady spotted her and beckoned her over.

'Sit next to me, Kate. I kept a free seat in case you turned up. Although, I didn't really expect to see you here, you having just arrived in the village.' She eyed Kate speculatively. 'You didn't say anything about coming when you brought Jess back.'

'No. I wasn't sure I was going to make it. But — well, I do live here now, after all, so the problems of the village could be said to be mine.' A couple of darting glances, a turn of the head, discovered no sign of Fergal. Yet, if he was the one responsible for organising the meeting, he'd have to be here — surely?

'Looking for someone?' Irene asked. 'Who told you about the meeting? I would have mentioned it, but I didn't want you to feel coerced into coming. As I said, it's early days yet for you.'

'I met Fergal Cameron this morning, walking his dog — Sam, isn't it? He and Jess seemed to know each other rather well.'

'You didn't tell me that either. So,

you got talking and Fergal asked you along, did he?' Irene's glance was a keen one now; knowing, even.

'Yes. I thought — well, why not?'

'What did you think of him?' Irene eagerly asked.

'Fergal?' Irene nodded. 'He seemed friendly enough — eventually. A bit cold to start with.'

'Yes, yes, but what did you think of him? Really? As one girl to another?' And she nudged Kate in the ribs.

Kate grinned. 'He seemed OK.' She shrugged, puzzled. Irene seemed very interested in Kate's feelings about someone whom she'd only spoken to for a couple of moments at the most. Was he a nephew? The son of a close friend?

Before she could ask, however, Irene threw back her head and hooted with mirth. 'OK? That's the last description I'd have given of Fergal. Go on,' the pale blue eyes gleamed wickedly at Kate, 'admit it; you thought he was downright gorgeous, didn't you? That's the main reason you're here, isn't it?'

49

Kate decided it would be safer to ignore the assumption that she was romantically interested in Fergal. She didn't think Irene would believe any sort of denial in any case. She'd got it into her head that Kate was only here because of Fergal and that was that. 'You obviously know him well.'

'Oh yes. He and his family have lived here for years.'

'Family?' That sounded as if he was married. So in that case, why was Irene seeming to foster some sort of romantic alliance?

'Him and his parents.'

'Oh. He's not married then?'

'No. Does that matter?' This time, the look was a speculative one.

'Of course not. I'm merely interested, as one villager about another. Nothing more, I can assure you.'

'I see.' Irene gave her a searching glance. 'Well, seeing as you're interested.' Irene's eyes once more danced, this time with open mischief. It was more than evident that she didn't believe Kate's assertion of impartiality, 'His parents retired to Scotland a couple of years ago. Fergal's Scottish by descent as you'll probably have deduced from his name. He took over the house from his parents — well, bought them out at market value, actually. It was his grandparents who originally moved down here from Inverness, for work reasons. Fergal's never been married.'

'Really. But he must be . . . '

'Thirty-seven or thirty-eight? Something like that. I've forgotten exactly.' She snorted, 'One of the penalties of getting old. The memory goes for dates,' she responded in answer to Kate's enquiring gaze.

'And he's never been married?' She raised an eyebrow.

'Well, just to satisfy your interest,' she emphasised the word, 'he's had a few relationships over the years — none of them lasted, mind you,' she gave Kate another searching glance. 'But that's because Fergal's not one to settle for second best.'

How on earth does she know that? Kate wondered.

'And if you're wondering how I know that . . . I was great friends with his grandparents and then his parents, especially his mother, and I've known Fergal since he was a baby. So I can assure you, with the utmost confidence, that he just hasn't met the right woman yet. When he does, I guarantee he won't waste any time in marrying her.'

'Hey, Kate. I wondered if I might see you here. Shame there isn't a seat otherwise I'd join you'

'Hello Dan.' This was from Irene.

'How are you, Mrs Willoughby?'

'Oh, you know. When the arthritis isn't playing up, I'm quite fine. Clearly, I don't need to introduce you to each other.'

'No. Kate and I have already met.'

He glanced smilingly down at Kate. 'Haven't we?'

'Yes, and it's nice to see you again.'

And it was, Kate decided. He had been the first person to welcome her to the village and it was good to have a friend, albeit one she hadn't been entirely honest with. A pang of guilt pierced her. She'd been less than honest with both of her new friends. She eyed Irene. The elderly woman was beaming at Dan.

'Sorry there aren't any spare seats. I'm sure you'd like to sit next to Kate,' she went on with a twinkle.

Really, Kate mused, she couldn't seem to help herself. She was now seemingly pushing her towards Dan — just moments after singing Fergal's praises. What was she? The village matchmaker?

Dan grinned back at her. 'That's OK, I'll stand over at the side.'

With that, a man sitting on the other side of Irene stood up. 'You can have this seat, mate. I've just spotted a friend,' and he drifted away.

'Oh, good — sit down, Dan,' Irene swiftly invited.

Dan grinned and readily did so. 'Well, that was convenient. It also means that I'm here — with the two best looking women in the room.'

'Tssk.' Irene pretended to be annoyed. 'Flattery will get you nowhere, young man.'

'So,' once Dan had taken his seat, he leant forward and asked Kate, 'how are things going at Bower Cottage?'

'Very well. The alterations I wanted to do are under way.'

'Alterations? You didn't say . . . '

'No, but I'm having the kitchen and bathroom redone.'

'Don't blame you. I always thought that kitchen needed brightening up. Who's doing it for you?'

Kate told him.

He looked surprised. 'And they could do it this quickly? The last time I wanted anything done by them, I had to wait weeks. But then . . . ' he eyed her knowingly, 'I'm not an extremely beautiful young woman.'

Kate blushed. 'I don't think it was that. Someone had cancelled on them and they could slot me in.' She wouldn't tell him that she'd agreed to pay a hefty bonus if the work was completed in double-quick time. That was no-one's business but her own, but still, she was beginning to wish she hadn't started this deceit. Dan and Irene were both so nice, so friendly and open, she felt as if she were betraying them. Maybe she should tell them, right now, and ask them to keep it to themselves? She was sure they would.

But even as she had the thought, Irene asked him, 'Have you seen Nicky lately?' and the moment was gone. 'Where is it he lives with his mother? My memory — I've forgotten.' She clicked her tongue in exasperation at herself.

'Wales. I've just got back, actually — from visiting.' Dan gave Kate a sideways smile; a slightly sheepish smile, it was true. 'My son — '

'I wish you'd mentioned going away when you said you'd see me in the pub one night.' She spoke lightly, so that he wouldn't take her remarks as any sort of rebuke. After all, his son was more important than meeting her for a drink. 'I duly went along and ended up on my own.' She pulled a face. 'Not something I want to repeat. It might give me the wrong sort of reputation.'

'Sorry about that, but Janet, my ex-wife, rang to say she and Nicky were off to Spain on holiday for a month, so if I wanted to see him before they went I'd better go. I should have phoned you. Look, excuse me, will you, Kate? Irene? I've just seen someone I want to talk to.'

'I've embarrassed him,' Irene said. 'Me and my big mouth. He probably wanted to tell you himself. So how did you meet him? I know he's your neighbour, but his house isn't that close.'

'He called in the day I arrived to introduce himself. He brought a bottle of champagne.'

'That was nice of him. But then, that's Dan — no money but a good heart.'

'Yes,' Kate watched him go, 'I like him.

It'll be good to know he's just along the lane.'

'A lovely looking girl like you? You'll have half the young men in the village calling round, I shouldn't wonder. There's a singular lack of unattached women around here.'

'Oh, I see.' She was still watching Dan. 'What happened between him and his wife?'

'She left him. Not his fault. He was a devoted husband and father. Sadly, someone with more charm came along — and with even more money, a lot more, and enticed her away. She simply upped and left, completely out of the blue, taking Nicky with her. The poor man was inconsolable for a long time, but I'm glad to say he's turned a corner now.' She eyed Kate. 'You could be just the diversion he — '

A loud buzz of voices drowned Irene out and Kate turned her head to see what had caused it.

'And here's Fergal,' Irene murmured in her ear.

Sure enough, the man Kate had met earlier was striding in, with the natural confidence of a born leader, glancing neither to the right nor left, as he took up his position on the platform at the front of the hall and started to speak.

Kate Joins The Protest

Precisely one week later, and still barely able to credit that she was actually doing this, Kate found herself at Box Wood, sitting alongside Irene, loosely roped to several other people, and facing a battalion of policemen, all armed with riot shields and batons.

This sort of thing wasn't her scene at all. Not like Fergal. She darted a glance at him, striding around in that self-assured manner that he had, for all the world as if it was something he did every day of his life: directing, organising his small band of troops. She didn't know whether to admire that or be irritated by it. Such confidence could often be a mark of arrogance.

She looked over at Dan. He was in the process of roping himself to a particularly stout-looking tree. It would be fair to say, he wasn't as good looking as Fergal, but, on the other hand, he was a much warmer, much more likeable character. Someone, in fact, whom you would be pleased to count as a friend. She couldn't imagine ever regarding Fergal as a friend, he was far too aloof; too unapproachable.

She'd gone to the local pub again, hoping to see Dan, and this time he'd been there. He'd kept his promise to introduce her to everyone. In fact, by the end of the evening she reckoned she'd met almost all of the village's residents and was drowning beneath the sheer number of names she'd now be expected to remember.

She'd seen nothing more of Fergal, not since the protest meeting the week before. She'd spotted him in the distance a couple of times on her walks with Jess, but he hadn't made any attempt to come over and speak — of course, he might not have seen her.

Either that, or he didn't wish to encourage any sort of friendship between them. Well, he could please himself.

His behaviour simply reinforced her opinion of overly good-looking men. They were far too full of themselves; too aware of their powers of attraction. She'd made enough friends in the village to not need him.

In any case, she hadn't needed to speak to him to find out all about him. She had her very own hotline directly into his life: Irene.

For all her denials of being a gossip, Irene had, and without any prompting from Kate, been more than ready to fill her in during their frequent coffee sessions together. Just as Kate had hoped, their friendship was rapidly developing, the very considerable age gap between them proving no obstacle to their increasing closeness.

'He plays his cards very close to his chest, does Fergal — and he's never been one to parade what he's got so — ' Irene had shrugged, 'who really knows what he's worth? He could be extremely hard up, I suppose. Although he does own a string of garages with car showrooms attached, as well as a couple of upmarket hotels and a recently acquired building business, so that would seem unlikely.'

Kate struggled to hide her amusement. How on earth did Irene know all this? Had Fergal told her? His parents? Or had the village tom-toms been busy? She recalled Dan warning her about that the first time they'd met.

'How long has Dan been out of work?'

'Not sure. A few months? Jobs are few and far between around here, especially the sort of job he had, that of bank manager. He might need to move to find something.'

Kate felt a surge of dismay. She hoped not. She was beginning to like Dan very much. Although, she was in no hurry to attach herself to anyone in particular. And really, how could she — with such a huge secret? Her spirit sank. What an uncomfortable corner she'd so heedlessly painted herself into. If she told the truth now — what were her friends going to think? Maybe she should have kept her distance, not allowed herself to grow so close to people so quickly?

She wondered then if that was why Fergal kept himself to himself? He certainly wasn't seen round and about in the village, at least, not by her — and she visited almost every day, to pick up a newspaper if nothing else; also Jess enjoyed the walk every bit as much as Kate did. Could it be that he was frightened of being pursued solely for whatever wealth he possessed? She hadn't as yet seen him with a woman, but then, as she'd just reflected, she'd barely seen him at all. Maybe he conducted his social life elsewhere? Somewhere a bit more sophisticated? With companions whose wealth and position matched his own? She glanced across at him now, chaining himself to a strategically positioned tree, directly in the path that the bulldozers would be forced to take to clear the woodland for the road.

Whatever else he was, he certainly

wasn't afraid to place himself in the firing line. She couldn't help feeling a tiny pang of admiration. She could see the bulldozers from where she was sitting, each vehicle and driver patiently waiting for the police to clear the protesters away.

One of the policemen began to speak. 'If you will please all peacefully leave, there'll be no trouble. We don't want to arrest you, but we will if we have to.'

'Huh!' Irene snorted at Kate's side. 'That's Johnny Brown. Knew him when he was running round in a nappy. Let him just try and move me.'

Kate laughed, just as a series of boos and catcalls rang out from the trees. A band of eco-warriors had set up camp in the branches of several of the more substantial trees a few days ago. Betty, who had joined Kate and Irene, had told her that a lot of them moved from protest site to protest site. 'Professional protesters,' she'd laughingly said. 'Still, we'll be glad of their support when push comes to shove, won't we?'

Kate had meekly agreed. Now, the laughter vanished and a stab of misgiving pierced her. Supposing she was arrested? And Irene? The protesters would be accustomed to that. And, for all her dislike of open confrontation, even she would survive it, hopefully unscathed.

But Irene was an old lady, despite her liveliness and valiant spirit. For the first time then, Kate felt genuine fear for her friend.

'Irene, do you think this is wise? I mean, at your age.'

'What!' Irene scoffed. 'I wouldn't miss this for anything. It's been a long time since I had so much fun. And don't you be so cheeky, my girl. At my age, indeed. I've a few years of fight left in me yet, I can assure you.'

Kate gave up and instead braced herself for a possibly violent confrontation. The police meant business; she could see. And after Fergal, she, Irene and Betty were amongst the first in line to be moved, forcibly or otherwise.

The Arrival Of Visitors

'Ok,' the police spokesman called. 'You've had long enough to leave.' He swung and faced his men. 'Right, men. Clear the way — now.'

With batons raised and riot shields held protectively before them, the policemen moved in a solid line towards the protesters.

Kate clung to Irene, Irene unashamedly clung to her, Betty hung onto Irene. They must make a pretty comical sight, Kate suspected. 'Make it as difficult for them as you can,' Irene told Kate. 'They have to be shown they can't just bulldoze over us.' Which was an unfortunate choice of words, given that the large vehicles were standing ready to do just that.

But, despite their valiant defiance, the protesters proved no match for the men who simply lifted them to their feet and then marched them towards the waiting police vans. There was nothing they could do but go. Once there, they were unceremoniously dumped inside, to sit, still roped together, while others were brought along and heaved in. Fergal and Dan were amongst them.

'Sorry, Fergal,' Irene said, 'we did try, didn't we, girls?' She glanced from Kate to Betty, her smile a rueful one. She looked back at Fergal. 'How did they get you unchained? You looked a permanent fixture to me.'

'Cutters. They sliced through the metal like a knife through butter.'

Kate felt more shaken than she cared to admit. She'd never taken part in anything even remotely resembling this before. It hadn't been a pleasant experience; anything but, in fact, and she wouldn't be in a hurry to repeat the ordeal.

'Are you OK?' Fergal was speaking directly to her and Irene now.

She gave a shaky smile, saying, 'I'm fine,'

Irene snorted, 'Huh! Take a lot more than that to deter me.'

'I expect you're sorry you agreed to help now?' His question this time was aimed solely at Kate.

'Of course, she's not,' Irene stoutly put in. 'Kate's made of sterner stuff than that.'

'Well, I would certainly hope so,' Dan put in.

Kate's glance at him was an enquiring one.

'You know, living in that cottage, all alone,' he explained. 'A lot of women wouldn't care for that. Too isolated.'

'Never mind,' Fergal said, 'You've got Dan right next door.' Although his words sounded as if they were meant to be reassuring, something in his tone made Kate think that he meant the exact opposite.

She stared at him, puzzled. He stared back, his expression unfathomable beneath heavy eyelids. She was tempted to ask him what he meant but as Dan was sitting, practically shoulder to shoulder with him, she decided that such a question would be fruitless. He'd hardly air any dislike that he had of Dan, with the subject of that emotion at his side.

They were all eventually transported to the police station at Oxbridge, where, after being left to cool their heels for half-an-hour or so, their ropes were untied and they were allowed to go.

'Don't worry,' Fergal assured them as they awaited taxis to take them all home, 'it will take them a lot longer to dislodge the eco-warriors from the trees. They're well and truly settled in, and once they pull up their rope ladders — well, it should prove almost impossible to reach them. However, if anyone's prepared for a second confrontation, they'll be more than welcome to join me in repeating today's actions tomorrow — so to speak.'

'Count me in,' Dan told the group at large. Kate said nothing.

As she'd already speculated, she wasn't sure she could summon up the fortitude to do this all over again another day. But Irene wasn't having that.

'Count Kate and me in.'

Kate's spirits plummeted.

Such self-sacrifice didn't prove necessary, however — to her heartfelt relief. Because she suspected that if everyone else had been going along again, Irene, in particular, she would have felt duty-bound to join in. It was Irene who rang to tell her that work had been called off for the present, to give the road builders and the police chance to work out the best way to get rid of the tree dwellers.

For now, the village, Box Wood — and Fergal's garden — was safe.

★   ★   ★

Kate had decided to tackle her garden herself. More satisfying that way, she'd decided, than hiring a team of experts. And without a job, she had plenty of time, after all. First though, she needed to buy herself the appropriate tools. She'd brought some along with her, but they'd been her father's and were looking extremely well used, to the point of decrepitude, in fact.

She needed to replace them; in particular, the spade and the hoe. Her father had always maintained that you couldn't do a good job with poor tools. Yet, he'd carried on using these. She smiled fondly, recalling how he'd given her her own small plot in the garden when she was just eight years old, and the way in which he'd patiently helped her plant sunflower and marigold seeds.

She sighed, shaking herself free of the poignant memories and instead rang Irene, intending to ask her advice on the best place to go and buy the necessary tools. Irene, however, was out so she decided to try Dan instead.

'I'll come with you,' he instantly offered. 'You'll need someone to carry things for you.'

They went in Kate's car; it was a small hatchback, perfect for carrying her purchases home. It was a bit shabby and she fully intended to treat herself to a new one, but she simply hadn't got round to it.

Dan glanced around the interior.

'Run OK, does she? Do you know, I'd have had you down as a sports car girl. You know, something sleek.'

'Huh, I wish,' Kate riposted.

She felt Dan's gaze resting on her, sensed his curiosity. 'Buying the cottage left you short, did it?'

Kate chose not to answer that question. Her personal finances were no-one's business but her own; they certainly weren't Dan's. Instead, she concentrated on pulling out safely onto the busy main road. Aside from her desire for privacy, she didn't want to tell yet more lies. And if she responded, that's exactly what she would have to do.

She could hardly say that she was trying to avoid giving the impression of great wealth, which, if she purchased an expensive sports car on top of buying the cottage, was precisely what she would do.

Dan seemed to accept her silence, however, and didn't press the matter, merely saying, 'Next left and then next right.' But then, it was as if he couldn't help himself. 'A mate of mine's got a TVR — open top, you know. He wants to sell. His wife's having a baby and he's buying a saloon — more room. Interested?'

'A TVR. That might be a bit beyond my means.'

'Oh, I thought — ' He stopped, as if he'd said more than he intended.

'What?' Kate slanted a gaze at him.

'Well — ' He shrugged. 'What with you buying the cottage and all you've done inside, I assumed money wasn't a problem.'

He was certainly persistent, she'd give him that. He was clearly determined to get the truth of her circumstances out of her. But Kate was equally determined that he wouldn't.

'It isn't as such.' Kate chose her words with care. This was exactly what she'd feared. 'But I do have my future to think about and I don't want to fritter my inheritance away.'

★　★　★

Kate started on the garden the next day, after gently and tactfully turning down Dan's offer of help. He was starting to make a few too many assumptions about her; assumptions that were a bit too near the truth for comfort. She'd maybe place a bit more distance between them — for a little while, at any rate. Although, how could she allow herself to eventually grow closer to him without telling him the truth? She couldn't, of course, she agonised.

'I'd really like to do it myself, Dan,' she'd told him, 'if you don't mind. That way I can take my time. As a rank beginner, I do need to work things out as I go. With someone else hurrying things along, I might not achieve the effect I want.'

But after three hours of cutting back and digging, and with a back that felt as if someone had taken a sledge hammer to it, she conceded that maybe she'd been a bit hasty turning down Dan's kind offer.

She straightened up with a groan, deciding enough was enough. She was a beginner, after all, and had very little experience of such hard physical labour. There was another day tomorrow and another one after that and so on; there was no rush. With that thought in mind, she ran herself a bath and was soaking in the hot, scented water, half asleep, when her front door bell rang.

She groaned softly — the last thing she wanted was company. If it was Dan, come to see how she was getting on — well, he'd get short shrift. She was too weary even for him. Reluctantly, she climbed out of the water and wrapped a dressing gown around herself before padding to the small window that overlooked the front entrance. She opened it and leant out, almost falling out when she saw who it was. It was Fergal. She'd expected to see anybody but him. What on earth could he want?

'Oh — um, Fergal. What a surprise.'

'I wanted a quick word, but if you're otherwise engaged . . . ' he began. His tone was cool to the point of indifference.

'It's OK. Give me five minutes — the door's on the latch. Just come in. I won't be long.'

Once back in her bedroom, she pulled on a T shirt and pair of jeans. A glance in the mirror showed her hair that was damp and dishevelled and a pair of cheeks that were still rosy pink from the warmth of the bath. She dragged her fingers through her hair, straightening it as best as she could.

She ran down the stairs. 'Right, here I am. Now what can I do for you?'

'It's about the people camping at Box Wood.'

'Oh?'

'They're starting to run short of supplies, you know, food — and I've been going round asking local people to help them out. Maybe have them in for a cooked meal; a bath now and again.

Let them do their laundry. They're a nice crowd for all their way-out looks and, without them, the wood would be in serious danger of being felled. I feel it's the least we can do.'

'Of course I'll help out. What did you have in mind?'

'A meal for half-a-dozen of them this evening.' He glanced around the gleaming and obviously brand new kitchen. 'You have been busy. In here and in the garden.' He indicated the depressingly small square of freshly dug ground outside, which had been all she'd had the strength to do.

'Well, I wouldn't say it's any sort of show place yet, but I'm pleased with the kitchen. It was only finished yesterday so yes, I'd be happy to try it all out.'

'That's marvellous.' He paused. 'Do you think the girls in particular could have a bath?'

She squashed the uncharitable thoughts that raced through her mind — namely, several very graphic images of her spanking new and very expensive bathroom being absolutely ruined by a horde of unruly youngsters. 'Of course. Tell them all to come round at six o'clock or thereabouts. I'll make sure there's plenty of hot water. They can bring their laundry too.'

'Thank you.' He gave her the sort of smile guaranteed to persuade her to do whatever he asked, ruined bathroom or no ruined bathroom. The sort that she recalled from their first meeting, the one that, even if she hadn't already agreed to attend his protest meeting, would have convinced her to do just that.

So, he was human after all. It was just a pity he didn't display that side of himself more often, instead of that cool, forbidding look that he seemed to favour. Still, it didn't stop her from wondering if he was also planning to entertain the protesters? From what Irene had said, his house was the height of luxury and elegance. Not the sort of place you'd want a horde of youngsters invading, she would have thought.

That evening six young people duly arrived, with Dan bringing up their rear. Kate couldn't help but be pleased to see him — despite her recent resolve to place a temporary distance between them.

A Disturbing End To The Evening

'The jungle drums let me know what was happening here, so, when I saw them all trooping past my place, I thought it might be advisable if I came too,' Dan murmured, as he followed the six young people in. 'I hope you don't mind?'

'No, I'm glad to see you.' And she was; she really was. The more she'd thought about it, the less she'd relished the idea of spending the entire evening in the company of complete strangers — despite her willingness to do what she could to help them in what must be extremely uncomfortable circumstances.

She wouldn't want to spend a single day, let alone weeks or even months, occupying the branches of trees. She admired them for their stoicism, their sheer determination, as they fought to preserve the precious countryside from the onslaught of the many developers and road planners whose sole ambition seemed to be to destroy it in the continual search for profit — or, as they deemed it, progress.

At the sound of the visitors, Jess bounded in from the garden where she'd been ecstatically engaged in familiarising herself with the many unfamiliar and different scents and smells. Kate had collected her from Irene late that afternoon after Fergal's visit, when she'd walked to the village for extra supplies of food. It had been a visible struggle for Irene to suppress her emotions upon having to part with her pet.

'Irene,' Kate had gently said, 'if you want Jess to stay with you just say the word. As I said in the beginning, I'll come and walk her for you each day.'

'No, no.' Irene had sniffed back the tears and energetically blown her nose. 'I've said she's too much for me and I meant it. It's not just the walking. She's brimful of energy all the time. It's best she goes with you. Two young things together. You'll suit each other admirably.'

Kate had eventually left, with Jess securely on her lead — just in case she took it into her head to go running back to Irene's — her emotions every bit as heightened as Irene's had been.

Now, not knowing who to go to out of so many, Jess plumped herself down and gazed around in bewilderment. It was the quietest she'd been since Kate had brought her home.

Dan looked startled. 'Isn't that Irene Willoughby's dog? What's she doing here?'

'She was getting too much for Irene, you know, exercising her and so on, so I offered to have her. She'll be company for me. As you pointed out, I am rather isolated here.'

'Oh, Lord! I didn't mean to make you nervous, Kate.' Dan looked appalled at his tactlessness. 'I could come round any time. You only need to phone me.'

'I know, Dan, but I don't want to impose too greatly on your good nature. You have your own life to lead. And I mean, you've come round this evening. I'm really grateful, but Fergal has assured me that they are perfectly decent people.'

'Hah! Fergal.' He snorted disparagingly. 'What would he know? Of course, he would tell you they're respectable. He wants to keep them at Box Wood. It's him and his garden that will be most affected by this road, after all. It suits him to get them fed and looked after. I think he's got a cheek asking you. I mean, you've only just arrived and already he's making demands. Why doesn't he have them at his place?'

His attitude surprised her, even though he was echoing her own questions. It also made her recall Fergal's attitude towards him. What had made these two men so hostile to each other? A woman? Had they been rivals at some time for a woman's attention?

And was Dan now afraid that she was attracted to Fergal? Should she reassure him that he had no need to worry? That she had no intention of getting involved with someone like Fergal. But would that be presumptuous of her?

After all, she didn't know for sure that Dan was romantically interested in her. He hadn't actually said so. 'Maybe he does? And it doesn't suit him to keep them there,' she pointed out. 'Everyone at that end of the village will suffer from noise, as well as pollution, if the road goes ahead.'

'You're right, of course. But still, he shouldn't be risking your safety and well-being. That's why I've come along — to keep an eye on things.'

'Well, you're very kind and there's more than enough food for one extra.'

As she had suspected she would, she quickly found herself thankful for Dan's company. Not one of the four lads and two girls was a day over nineteen, and, although she was only six years their senior, she felt positively ancient by comparison. Their talk was all about pop singers and their life in the camp. She had nothing in common with them, whatsoever.

One of the young men, however, did succeed in endearing himself to her. He introduced himself as Bush Patterson.

'Is that your real name — Bush?' she asked.

'Nah. It's Brian. I changed it to Bush — seems more fitting somehow, with my way of life.'

'Well,' Kate smiled, 'I can't dispute that.'

Bush presented a slightly more conventional appearance than the others. His hair was cut shorter as well as being tidier and his beard was neatly trimmed, and he had the most amazing eyes Kate had ever seen. A deep navy blue with the sort of long, curling lashes that most of the women that Kate knew would kill to possess.

'Thank you for this,' he said. 'I saw you at the demonstration the other day.'

Kate was belatedly aware of Dan's

gaze upon them. The other young people had migrated into the garden and were loudly discussing the amount of work that Kate still had to do.

'We could give you a hand out there, as a thank you for tonight.'

'There's no need for that,' Dan chipped in. Kate chewed at her bottom lip. Her earlier doubts about his romantic interest in her were banished with those five words. The only trouble was that his possessiveness over her was also becoming apparent and she wasn't sure she welcomed that. It could indicate a jealous nature — which would go some way towards explaining his hostility towards Fergal.

What it didn't explain was Fergal's attitude to him. It certainly couldn't be any sort of jealousy over her. Fergal hadn't exhibited any kind of romantic interest in her. Far from it. 'I'm perfectly willing to give Kate a hand.'

'Kate.' Bush smiled slowly at her. 'It suits you. Is that just Kate or is it Katherine?'

'Just Kate.' Just as she'd sensed Dan's interest in her, so she now perceived Bush's attraction to her. Flattering. Considering he couldn't be much more than nineteen. 'But feel free if you want to have a go at some digging,' she said impetuously.

She couldn't mistake Dan's hurt at her words. Oh Lord! She'd turned down his offer of help and now, here she was, accepting Bush's at their first meeting. In an effort to make amends, she said, 'You supervise, Dan, while I finish dinner. Oh, by the way, Bush,' she swung to the younger man again and was amused to find him still gazing at her, 'there's loads of hot water if anyone wants a bath.'

★　★　★

After a bit of a sticky start, the evening eventually turned into an enjoyable one. A couple of the lads had bought guitars with them and after they'd polished off the beef casserole that Kate had prepared, they began to play them, encouraging everyone to sing along. Only Dan stayed silent. It made Kate feel uncomfortable.

The last thing she'd wanted to do was hurt his feelings. But the fact was that Bush had made no secret of his admiration for her, taking every opportunity to sit by her, helping her with the clearing of the dishes, the loading of the dishwasher. As a result of this, Kate suspected, Dan had begun to dog her every step — especially if they happened to be going in the same direction as Bush's.

'I'll do that,' he'd insist.

Bush winked at her once or twice. Kate tried to ignore him, but eventually Dan noticed it and his expression hardened. In the end, he lost patience and bluntly pointed out, 'It's getting late. Isn't it time you all left?'

'Dan!' Kate exclaimed. She understood his annoyance, but Bush was just a boy and she was disinclined to tell him to leave her alone. He'd soon lose interest once he realised Kate didn't return his feelings. In any case, she was too old for him.

However, despite her annoyance at Dan's presumption in telling everyone to leave — it was her house, after all, and therefore her prerogative to indicate when everyone should make their departure — Kate had to admit she was thankful when everyone finally went.

Dan, she was sure, had only been thinking of her. It felt good, as a matter of fact, to have a man watching over her, caring about her. It was a feeling she hadn't experienced in a long time. She'd been too busy fending for herself since her mother died to have any time for a serious relationship.

Her mother hadn't left much behind her upon her premature death, other than a substantial amount of debt. Kate hadn't realised how much her mother had been spending, but there'd been a credit card statement for an amount that that had truly horrified Kate.

An amount that she'd have to settle.

Eighty pounds altogether at the local hair salon, a hundred and five pounds for groceries, almost a hundred and fifty pounds for petrol, five hundred and eighty pounds for clothes, and so on, and all brought forward from previous months.

When Kate checked earlier statements, it was clear that her mother had been merely paying the minimum amount due each month, injudiciously staving off the inevitable day of reckoning.

Kate hadn't been aware of an excess of new clothes, but upon opening her mother's wardrobe, she'd found it crammed full of garments that she'd never seen before. Garments she was sure her mother had never worn. She'd donated it all to a local charity shop and eventually, by dint of severely curbing her own spending, had managed to pay it all off. Clearly her mother had sought to assuage her grief over her husband's death by indulging in spending sprees.

Kate hadn't been surprised, not when she thought about it; her parents had loved each other deeply. She'd sometimes wondered whether her mother had really needed anyone else, other than her husband, especially and, at times, extremely troublesome daughter. More than once, Kate had felt like a spare part, an unwanted third person; an outsider, even. Oh, they'd loved her, her father certainly had, but she'd sensed, even at a young age, that they'd loved each other more.

Even so, the sense of loss that Kate had experienced upon her mother's death, the sense of sheer loneliness and vulnerability, had been overwhelming. Her answer had been to keep herself busy, selling the house, most of the furniture, she'd kept one or two pieces in memory of them, and by working all hours that God sent. She didn't know what she'd have done without Sally. She'd proved the one steadying force in Kate's life. Why, they'd even managed to get jobs in the same place. Which was why Sally's behaviour in the wake of her lottery win had been so hurtful; traumatic, even. She still found it hard to credit that someone could change so dramatically, and so swiftly.

Kate had never known the sort of love which her parents had shared. Had no concept, in fact, of how that felt. But now, she sensed that something was about to blossom between her and Dan, and she welcomed that.

It was more than time that she gave some consideration to her future. A future that she wanted to share with someone, and Dan, she decided, could well prove to be that someone. He was thoughtful, kind — tender, even. The sort of man who would make an ideal husband.

'Come on, Jess,' she called now, 'bedtime.'

She'd decided to let Jess sleep on the floor by the side of her bed. After Dan's remarks about the dangers of her isolation — something she was becoming increasingly aware of — she thought she'd probably feel better that way. As she did every night, she turned out lights, checked doors and windows, and then more wearily than usual climbed the stairs to her room. She was lying in bed reading a book — something she made a habit of doing as she'd found she slept more soundly afterwards — when she and Jess heard the sound from outside. The unmistakable squealing of the garden gate.

$\star$ $\star$ $\star$

Once she'd been down and thoroughly checked the garden, she decided to make herself a hot drink before returning to bed. Something to soothe her jangling nerves. Hot milky chocolate. It was a drink her mother had always made for her if she'd been upset or frightened by a bad dream. It had always worked, calming her fears, her distress.

She just hoped it still did, because the thought of having someone standing in the dark, in the garden, watchful and unmoving, was a disturbing one. As she made the drink, something occurred to her. Could the intruder have been one of the eco-warriors? Bush, maybe? Perhaps he'd thought he'd left something behind?

Yet, she'd found nothing that hadn't belonged to her when she'd tidied up before going to bed. Of course, it could also have been Dan, concerned over her welfare — or maybe, to check that Bush hadn't returned? She smiled to herself. He was certainly very keen to keep an eye on her. But wouldn't he have called up to her when she first appeared at the window? The same question applied to Bush? Either of them would have seen her, surely? And, just as surely, wouldn't they have knocked on the door? Why stand silently in the garden? Maybe she ought to call the police?

She decided to sleep on it. One thing she did know, however, she wouldn't mention it to Dan. Because she wouldn't put it past him to constantly call round. And as much as she liked him, she didn't want that — not yet.

By the next morning, she still hadn't made up her mind what to do. If she reported the intrusion, what action could the police take? They didn't have the manpower to put a watch on the house. And would she want that, in any case?

She'd let it go. Put it down to a one-off incident and hope that was an end to it. Because the more she thought about it, and about the way in which he'd behaved towards her that evening, possessively, the more convinced she became that it had been Dan, come back to check up on her.

He'd probably been too embarrassed to call up to her, or maybe frightened that she'd be annoyed with him. There had been one or two occasions the evening before when she hadn't been able to quite hide her irritation with his manner towards the young protesters and Bush, in particular.

Despite knowing he was only thinking of her safety and well-being.

But when Bush showed up later that morning, her conviction that the night-time intruder had been Dan wavered. The young man's admiration of her was even more pronounced than it had been the evening before.

She decided not to say anything to him — for fear of embarrassing him — but when she saw the manner in which Jess sniffed at him, growling deep in her throat as she had done the night before, she decided that the dog had recognised his smell from beneath the crab apple tree and her suspicion was confirmed. Mystery solved. She felt better immediately, more relaxed. A lovesick young man she could deal with.

'I thought I'd come and do some gardening for you,' Bush said. 'My way of repaying your kindness last night.'

'Oh Bush, there's no need for that.' Although, she wasn't about to turn down his offer. A hand with the digging that needed to be done would be more than welcome — as she'd discovered to her cost after her last stint with the spade. 'Aren't you needed at camp?'

'Nah! There's more than enough people there — me missing won't even be noticed. Now, where shall I start?'

It took just five minutes after that for Dan to arrive and Kate found herself wondering if he kept an eye out for anyone on their way to her house. Amusement flared, almost instantly giving way to confusion as she watched Jess go straight to Dan and go through precisely the same ritual as she had with Bush only moments before, making a complete nonsense of Kate's theory that the late night visitor had been Bush.

Dan followed her into the kitchen and his gaze immediately went to Bush beavering away in the back garden. 'I thought I saw him go past.'

'He's helping me with the digging, that's all.'

'I would have done that, Kate. I keep offering but you keep turning me down.' Wounded exasperation swiftly turned to concern. 'And I'm not sure you should be giving the run of your place to someone you don't know.'

'I'm not giving him the run of the place, Dan, merely the garden. And, anyway, I don't really know you either,' she gently pointed out.

'But that's different, surely? I live next door, I'm settled, people know me — I have a reputation here in the village. For goodness sake, I was the bank manager!' He was the very picture of wounded indignation.

Kate apologised. 'Yes, of course. I'm sorry, but — '

'But what?'

He was watching her intently, she noticed, as he waited for her to answer.

'Nothing. It's very good of you to look out for me.'

'But you don't want to grow too close too quickly.'

What was it with these village people? Irene was the same. Highly intuitive. Did they all go on some sort of mind reading course? She was beginning to suspect they did. Because they seemed to know what she was thinking almost before she did. It made her feel edgy; exposed. It wouldn't be long before one of them winkled out the truth about her — and then what would they think?

'That's OK. I prefer to take my time too. But I'm not offering you marriage, I'm simply offering to help you.' Dan's eyes, in spite of his reasonable tone, had narrowed, darkened. 'After all, once bitten, twice shy.'

He was referring to his broken marriage, of course. 'I'm sorry, Dan. It's just that Bush feels he's repaying me for cooking dinner for them all. I hadn't got the heart to say no.'

'Oh! So there is a heart then beneath that composed exterior?'

It was lightly said but, nonetheless, Kate perceived the underlying hurt.

'Sorry! All I'm doing this morning is apologising to you.' Dan gave a lame smile. 'Actually I came to ask you out for a meal this evening. I though maybe we could go to The Feathers.'

'I'm sorry.' And she truly was. 'But I'm going round to Irene's. She rang first thing this morning.'

'Oh, I see. Well, another time, then.'

★ ★ ★

Kate's next visitor was Fergal. Jess went through the identical procedure that she'd gone through with both Bush and Dan. It was obviously something that she was going to do with everyone who came to the house from now on. Could the events of late last night have had an adverse effect on Jess as well? Kate sighed.

It was increasingly obvious that her behaviour had no special significance, which meant she was none the wiser as to who had been in the garden last night. She'd put it down to a passing vagrant looking for somewhere to sleep and forget it, she resolved. It was either that or go mad with the worry of it all. And that, she steadfastly refused to do.

'Ah, I can see you're busy.'

'Not really. Though Bush certainly is.

Fancy a cool drink? We could take it in the garden. I'm sure Bush would join us.'

'I'm sure he would,' he drily said.

Kate stared at him. Was that irony? Sarcasm? Or was he also put out at the sight of Bush — there, working in her garden? Honestly, what was wrong with these men? Fergal had been the one to ask her to entertain the young people. Why should he now be vexed at seeing Bush helping her as a way of saying thank you? It didn't make sense. Dan's displeasure she could understand. He clearly was attracted to her.

But Fergal? As she'd already concluded, there'd been no indication of any sort of interest, romantic or otherwise. Why, he barely noticed her.

Deciding to disregard his manner, she asked, 'You're not at work today then?' as she headed for the fridge and the orange juice.

'No, I fancied a day off. I wondered if you'd like to have a spot of lunch with me?'

Good grief, Kate mused. Wasn't she the popular one? All of this attention could go to a girl's head. Irene's remark about the hordes of admirers she'd probably attract returned to her then. Somehow though, she couldn't picture Fergal as just one of many. He was far too arrogant. He was most likely simply being polite in return for her agreeing to his request to give dinner to some of the protesters.

'Well,' she cast a look in Bush's direction, 'it's a bit difficult today.' And she could hardly say yes to Fergal, even if it was for lunch rather than dinner, when she'd just turned Dan down.

'I see.' He spoke tersely. And Kate found herself wondering what, exactly, it was that he saw? 'Maybe another time then.'

Kate couldn't for the life of her imagine sitting down to a meal with this stony-faced individual. I mean — what on earth would they talk about? He was a high-powered businessman with his finger in several pies if Irene was to be believed, and here she was, ex-manager of a small cafe. Hardly in the same league.

No, Fergal would go for a woman of equal status — one of those frighteningly efficient businesswomen that were featured in the newspapers, or even on the television now and again.

The sort that expertly juggled a perfect family life with an equally perfect business life. They could talk profit and loss all evening then compare balance sheets. She only just stopped herself from yawning at the mere thought of it.

'How did you get on last night?' he asked, evidently dismissing her rejection of his invitation with little or no emotion. 'Everything go all right?'

'Of course.'

'Because I did wonder if I'd maybe been a bit presumptuous — asking you to share your home with a group of strangers. You being a newcomer so to speak.'

'Why should that prevent me from

being charitable?'

'Well, I was a little worried about you.'

'You needn't have been; Dan was here too.'

'Was he?' His expression changed, only fractionally, but enough for Kate to detect it. It was becoming more and more obvious that the two men really didn't like each other.

Something occurred to her then. Instead of Dan — could it have been Fergal standing in the garden? He'd been worried about her, he'd just said so. But he too would have knocked on the door, surely? If only to check she really was all right? And he'd certainly mention it now, wouldn't he? Maybe she should ask him? But what if it hadn't been him? And what if he should mention it to someone else? And it got back to Dan? He'd wonder why she hadn't told him — and then there'd be a repeat of that wounded outrage. No, best to say nothing — to anyone.

'Aah, well, if I'd known you'd

appointed him to be your watch-dog . . . ' She couldn't mistake the sarcasm this time.

'I didn't appoint him to be anything.' She was determined to set him straight. 'He just turned up. He was worried about me too, apparently.' Now it was her turn to be sarcastic.

Sadly, it didn't have the desired effect. Because, instead of looking suitably chastened, Fergal merely remarked, 'Well, as my fears have all been proved groundless, and you can't come to lunch, I'll bid you good day.'

And that was that. He left as suddenly as he'd appeared, and he hadn't even drunk the juice she'd poured for him.

An Evening Out
With Dan

Contrary to Kate's expectation that Jess's greeting would be the same whoever arrived, the next time Bush turned up at the cottage she took absolutely no notice of him, apart from the most cursory glance. The same thing happened when Dan appeared just moments later.

'What's he doing now?' He clearly was trying to sound amused rather than irritated at the sight of Bush once more labouring outside.

'He's digging me a pond.'

'I could have done that for you. I could even have got the use of a digger.'

'My word, you do have a lot of useful contacts, Dan,' Kate murmured. 'A friend who just happens to want to sell a sports car; now someone with a digger.'

She felt instant remorse as his mouth tightened and a tinge of red coloured his face. That had been unforgivable. What on earth was wrong with her? She wasn't usually so sharp-tongued. And Dan was only trying to help her, after all. 'I know you would have helped, Dan, but I'm sure you must have lots to do; not least, job hunting.'

'I've given up on that for the moment. There's nothing around.'

'I'm sorry to hear that. You said you were a bank manager?'

'Yes. They closed my branch and I — um, I didn't want to move to another. Could be that I'll have to, though.' His gaze lingered on her: warm, smouldering, almost. 'And that would be a shame.'

Kate couldn't mistake his meaning — now that she was here.

'Changing the subject completely, I've come to see if you're free this evening. I thought — dinner? Same place, The Feathers.'

Kate felt a spurt of pleasure. 'I'd like

that, but only if you'll let me go halves with the bill.'

'There's no need for that. I may be out of work, but I'm not totally broke.'

'No, I'm sure you're not, but as you've said yourself, there's no immediate job on the horizon.'

'Well, if you put it like that.' he grinned engagingly. Kate felt her heart miss a beat, making her question why she was so set on keeping him at arm's length.

As she'd already decided, he was everything she'd ever wanted. Attractive, warm, kind: every woman's dream, in fact. 'OK. I accept your generous offer,' and clearly without that misguided and, in her view, outdated male pride that so many men exhibited when a woman tried to put herself on an equal footing by paying half of the bill.

*   *   *

The Feathers, when they got to it that evening, was a sixteenth century coaching inn about ten or twelve miles outside of Great Mindon. Like Kate's cottage, it was a criss-cross of black beams and white walls, but without the added charm of a thatched roof. Dan told her it specialised in seafood of every description.

'Their crab is fantastic, when they've got it, that is,' he enthused. He took her by the elbow and led her into the restaurant. It was low ceilinged, heavily beamed, and consisted of a series of discreet alcoves, with only a candle on each table for light. It was the sort of place that oozed romance. Kate swallowed nervously.

Although, she'd more or less made up her mind that Dan was the man for her, was all this a bit — well, premature? She'd have liked to take things a bit more slowly.

For starters, he knew nothing of real significance about her. Namely, the fact that she was a millionairess. She chewed at her bottom lip. She shouldn't have agreed to come? Her doubts resurfaced. She needed to come clean about her circumstances before encouraging the hopes that he so obviously had with regards to her and a future together, and she simply wasn't ready to do that — not yet.

She continued to gnaw at her bottom lip. What on earth was she going to do? She knew she should tell her friends the truth but she was so afraid of losing their respect, their liking — which increasingly seemed the inevitable consequence of her deceit.

Why, oh why hadn't she been honest about it from the start? Now, she was caught in a trap entirely of her own making. She couldn't speak out for fear of upsetting everyone, but she couldn't embark upon a loving relationship without telling the truth.

The maître d' greeted Dan as an old friend and led them to one of the alcoves. From then on, Dan didn't behave at all like a man out of work. The dishes he selected from the menu meant that, even with Kate footing half of the bill, his share was going to come to a substantial amount.

Could he afford this? Maybe she should offer to pay for it all? But would he agree to that? Her fears were confirmed when at the end of the evening, the maître d' brought them the bill, and Dan proceeded to settle his half on his credit card.

'Dan . . . ' she began, 'I wouldn't mind paying the whole bill.'

'Certainly not.' He spoke indignantly. 'I don't ask a woman out for a meal and then expect her to foot the bill. It's bad enough having to accept half.'

Kate didn't press the matter and they left the restaurant and began to walk to where Dan had left his car in the restaurant's car park.

'So . . . ' he said, 'Great Mindon not proving too quiet for you then?'

'Anything but. There's always something going on. And now I've got Jess everything's working out well.'

'Aah, yes, Jess. She must make you feel more secure.'

'Yes, she does.'

'Although,' he smiled at her, 'I can't imagine she'd be much good as a guard dog. I mean, she's so docile, so — gentle.'

'Oh, you might be surprised there. Why, the other night after you'd all gone . . . ' Kate stopped. The only person she'd told about her nocturnal visitor was Irene and she'd fully intended keeping it that way. Irene, not surprisingly, had been shocked and had pressed her to report it to the police.

'It could have been anyone, Kate. A burglar looking for a way in. Really, you're not safe anywhere nowadays. I can remember when people used to leave their doors unlocked all the time. You can't do that now — even in a village like this.'

'It hasn't happened again and — well, I've been wondering if it could have been Dan — or maybe Bush, one of the eco-warriors who'd been to dinner. He did seem rather taken with me. Although he can't be much more than nineteen.'

Irene raised an eyebrow. 'A sort of

Romeo and Juliet situation — with a rather older version of Juliet, if you don't mind me saying, and a window instead of a balcony?' Clearly, Irene's mind worked in the same way that Kate's did. It seemed yet another bond forged between them. 'Seriously, Kate, you ought to report it.'

'Yes — after we'd gone — what? What happened?' Dan now exclaimed. 'I knew it, it's that wretched boy, isn't it? He came back, didn't he? I was right.'

'No, you weren't. It wasn't him — well, I don't think it was.'

She'd have to tell him what had happened now. He'd see through any attempt at prevarication. 'It was after I'd gone to bed. I heard a sound outside and got up to have a look. I saw some-one, just standing in the front garden — staring at the cottage'

'You what? What time was this?'

His anger did seem a little excessive in Kate's opinion. Nonetheless, his concern warmed her. It was comforting to know he cared. She no longer felt so alone. 'About elevenish.'

'I warned you. You need to be on your guard with people like that. You can bet it was him, that — that Bush. Stupid name!' He snorted contemptuously. 'I'd even be prepared to put money on the fact that it was him! He spent half the night gazing at you, following you around. It's disgusting.'

'No, it's not. It's rather sweet, actually. And he's been very helpful to me in the garden.'

'Yes, too blasted helpful,' he muttered. 'I find myself wondering what his ulterior motive is.'

'For heaven's sake, Dan, if it was him then I'm sure I've got nothing to worry about. Irene,' she grinned, desperately trying to lighten the tension, 'said it reminded her of Romeo and Juliet.'

'Humph! Ridiculous!. You know nothing about him. Have you asked him if it was him who was loitering outside, have you?'

'No, of course not.'

'Well, I will. In fact, I've a good mind to come round and sort him out.'

This sort of reaction was precisely what she had feared. 'Dan, Dan,' she sought to calm him down, 'it hasn't happened again. And if it does, I'll call the police — I promise. Now, please, just leave it to me to sort it out.'

'We-ell, OK. I'm not happy about it though, Kate.'

With his agreement grudgingly given, Kate breathed a sigh of relief. The last thing she wanted was Dan taking matters into his own hands.

'Look, if you're worried about anything, anything at all, you call me. Any time, day or night. Here's my card, with my mobile number printed on it. It's usually switched on. So — ' gradually, he was calming down, 'what did you do?'

'I had a look round outside, of course.'

'You went outside — alone.' He grasped hold of her hand and pulled her in to him. 'Anything could have happened. You could have been attacked!' His face paled. 'It doesn't bear thinking about.'

Kate stared up at him. He really did care about her. Why was she holding back? He was such a genuine man. Surely he'd understand why she'd been less than honest? All she had to do was tell him the truth.

'Oh, Kate,' he muttered, and before she had time to do anything, much less tell him the truth, he had pulled her close and was kissing her. A kiss that all too swiftly turned from a light brushing of lips into something much more passionate. Something that, for all her attraction to him, Kate wasn't ready for; not yet.

He must have sensed that because he released her instantly. 'Sorry — sorry. I didn't mean to do that — not yet.'

'It's OK.'

'No, it's not. Put it down to my fright over what you told me.' He gave a harsh laugh, but his face was still ashen.

'I wish I hadn't told you now,' she

lightly remarked.

'No, no. I'm glad you did. And my request still stands. Phone me — any time, night or day — you have nothing to fear from me, Kate. Honestly.'

Kate Begins To Feel Threatened

That night, it wasn't the squealing of the garden gate that disturbed Kate's slumber, it was Jess's low, rumbling growl at the side of her and then the quick movement as the dog got up and went downstairs. Half asleep still, she squinted at the clock. One o'clock? She sat up in bed and switched on the light, heart pounding and senses alert for whatever it was that had disturbed the dog.

She could hear nothing, but knowing she'd be unlikely to settle again until she'd checked that it wasn't a repetition of the other night, she climbed from her bed and walked to the window. As she had done then, she looked down, particularly at the shadows beneath the crab apple tree. There wasn't anyone there. She breathed a sigh of relief.

So what had disturbed Jess? Because something had. The animal normally didn't move all night.

She walked out onto the landing to see where her pet had gone.

'Jess,' she called, 'come on, girl.' When the dog failed to respond, Kate too went downstairs. 'There you are! What are you doing down here?'

Jess was sitting quite still, just inside the front door. On the floor in front of her was an envelope.

Kate walked across and picked it up. Her name was crudely printed on the front of it, just her Christian name: KATE.

With fingers that shook, she slit it open and pulled out a single sheet of paper. She read the words printed upon it.

I KNOW WHY YOU LEFT BIRMINGHAM AND CAME HERE. DON'T WORRY THOUGH. YOUR SECRET IS SAFE WITH ME — FOR NOW.

Kate's heart accelerated as her pulses throbbed sickeningly and she began to shake. This put the other night's intrusion into a whole new perspective. For it had to be the same person responsible for both incidents — surely?

Her first instinct was to tell someone. Dan. She ran to the phone and had the receiver in her hand before she slowly put it down again.

She'd been about to punch out his number when it occurred to her that she'd have to show him the note and then, as sure as night followed day, he'd want to know what the secret was. And, despite her longing to tell him, she was still unsure how he'd react. The last thing she wanted to do was lose his friendship. Especially now.

Kate read the words once more. YOUR SECRET IS SAFE WITH ME — FOR NOW. Whoever had written this knew about her lottery win. That was bad enough. But the final two words. Were they intended as some sort of threat? Maybe leading up to a demand for a share of the money in order to maintain the writer's silence?

★ ★ ★

The next morning she rang Irene and told her she was going to the police.

'Why? Has that man been back? Do you want me to come with you?'

'No — look, I'll call and see you after I've been there, if that's OK?'

Kate drove the short distance to Oxbridge and the police station. Having been taken there on the day of the protest, she had no trouble finding it again. She told the young constable on the desk about the letter and also about her late night visitor.

He didn't seem overly concerned about either and Kate wondered if she was maybe making too much of things. After all, she'd not been harmed in any way either time. Just frightened. And nothing had been damaged or stolen. And there'd been no real threat made against her, other than those final two words in the letter — FOR NOW. And could that justifiably be described as a threat?

'Have you brought the letter with you?'

'Yes.' Kate handed it over.

He read it and then looked up and asked, 'What does it mean? What is there to know about you? This secret?'

Kate had no option but to tell him; she asked him to keep her confidence, explaining how she'd been forced to leave her previous home and job.

'Well,' the constable looked at her thoughtfully, 'I'll have to put it in my report but what you've told me will remain strictly confidential, Miss Brookes. Apart from that, I really don't know what we can do.'

He scrutinised the words again.

'Are there any neighbours who might have seen anything — on either occasion?'

'No. I don't have a near neighbour. There is a Dan Peters who lives a couple of hundred yards along the lane.

He wouldn't be able to see the house or the garden.'

'And I take it he doesn't know about your lottery win?'

'No. I haven't told anyone at all.'

'Hmm. Well . . . ' He shrugged.

She was wasting his time. Two separate incidents — with no proven connection. What could the police do? He didn't say it, but Kate knew it was what he was thinking. Even so, she felt marginally better as she set off for Irene's. She'd taken Jess with her and, as it was a cloudy, cool day, had left her in the car while she was in the police station. Now, she took her in with her.

The dog, as always, was ecstatic at seeing Irene again and Kate was so taken up with preventing her from knocking the older woman over that it was several seconds before she noticed Fergal. Which, very effectively, put paid to Kate's intention of telling her friend the truth.

She'd been feeling increasingly guilty at lying to Irene and had decided that morning to come clean. Unlike Sally, Irene, she was sure, would respect her confidence.

Once she'd laughingly disentangled herself from Jess's enthusiastic embrace, Irene explained, 'Fergal's here to give me some advice on selling my car. I'm too old to drive; even with my glasses on my sight isn't good enough any more, and I was just telling him about your uninvited visitor the other night. And your visit to Oxbridge Constabulary. What was it this time? You said it wasn't the man again.'

Kate's thoughts raced. Now what? 'Oh, it was nothing really. I just had second thoughts and decided I ought to tell them.'

'Are you sure that's all it was?' Fergal put in. 'You look rather pale if you don't mind me saying so. Exhausted, in fact. Aren't you sleeping?'

'Not all that well, no — '

She saw Irene's look of sympathy and, for a split second, was sorely tempted to confide in them both. Especially when

Irene went on to say, 'Well, I'm not surprised after what's happened. It'd be enough to scare anyone.'

'Do you have any idea at all,' Fergal went on, 'who it might have been?'

'Well, to be honest, I did wonder about Bush.'

'Bush? Is that the lad who's helping you in your garden?'

Obviously Irene hadn't mentioned Kate's suspicion to Fergal. He looked astonished when she said, 'Yes.'

'Why do you think it was him? Did you recognise him?'

'No, but he — he, um — '

'He took a fancy to her,' Irene blurted.

Something glinted in Fergal's whisky-coloured eyes. For the first time, Kate noticed several minute gold flecks in them.

'I see.'

Kate felt her cheeks grow warm beneath his concentrated gaze. 'I don't know that — not for sure.' She glared balefully at Irene. This was all her fault.

Blurting out that Bush had taken a fancy to Kate.

'No offence intended, but isn't he a little young for you?' Fergal went on to demand.

Stung by his obvious scepticism about Bush's admiration of her, Kate's reply when it came was waspish. 'I didn't say I reciprocated.'

'Even so, as little as I know about him, I wouldn't have thought he would resort to hanging about your garden at the dead of night hoping for a glimpse of you. It's a little extreme, don't you think? Even for the most ardent admirer?'

'Oh, I don't know if it was him or someone else?' She was deliberately evasive.

Fergal saw through that straight away. 'Dan Peters, maybe?'

'No.' Kate was all indignation. Did he think that was why she leant out, barely half dressed? What did he think she was? The village trollop? She had her mouth open, ready to put him right, when he coolly interrupted her.

'If you want my opinion as to the identity of your night-time caller, look no further than him. He's always following you around like a puppy.'

'Why on earth should you think Dan would do something like that? I might as well think the same of you.'

'Feel free! But I can assure you, I've got better things to do with my time than hang around a woman.'

Irene smothered a chuckle before remonstrating, 'Don't be silly, Kate, Fergal would never do something like that.'

'Well, neither would Dan, I'm sure.'

'Are you?' Fergal said. 'He made a fool of himself once before with another woman, an Elizabeth Corbett, just a few months after Janet left him, actually. She was a young widow. He hung about her house, called in at all hours, sent flowers, notes . . . '

'Village gossip, Fergal,' Irene scoffed.

'Well, if that's all it was, why did she suddenly move away?'

'Because she wanted to?' Kate bit out. 'But even if it was true, it doesn't mean Dan would steal into my garden at the dead of night.' she protested.

Could that be the reason for the two men's hostility to each other? Fergal had also been interested in this Elizabeth Corbett and Dan, in his view, had driven her away? It was a possibility.

Dan could be a little — enthusiastic in his courting — as she'd also discovered. Such ardour, she was sure, could upset some women, scare them, even. Was that what had happened in this case? Well, if it was, she, Kate, was made of sterner stuff. She could handle Dan and there was no harm in him, she'd stake her life on that. He was simply concerned for her well-being and safety.

'Let's hope you're right,' Fergal drily put in. 'But it seems to me that Peters has a particular fondness for a beautiful woman that results in his better judgement deserting him — so be warned.'

Beautiful? Her heart lurched at his

insinuation that she was as beautiful as this Elizabeth Corbett apparently was. Maybe he wasn't quite as heedless of her as she'd thought? She wasn't sure how she felt about that.

'Why don't you invite Fergal and me over tonight to keep you company?' Irene quickly asked, distracting her from her somewhat disturbing reflections. 'Then if this — person puts in an appearance again, we can catch him, red-handed, so to speak.'

'And how does Fergal feel about that? I mean, he might find himself chasing someone out of my garden.'

Fergal shrugged. 'It's OK, I don't have anything else on.'

Well, that put her well and truly in her place. So much for her wondering if he'd noticed her more than she'd thought.

'I tell you what. Why don't I make you a meal? Now, what can I cook that would be especially tempting?' She put her head to one side, tapping her mouth with her index finger, pretending to give the matter lengthy and exaggerated consideration. 'I know! What about hemlock stew? With a side serving of deadly nightshade maybe? Hmm?'

Irene gave a snort of amusement. 'I think you've annoyed her, Fergal.'

Fergal raised an eyebrow. 'I can't imagine how.'

'Could it have anything to do with your lack of enthusiasm about the visit? I mean, you don't have anything else on. Really, Fergal!'

'Oh, I see. That was rather ungracious of me, wasn't it?' A rueful smile tugged at the corners of his mouth. 'What I actually meant was that I had no objection to being invited without being consulted first, it wasn't strictly an answer to the — '

'Fergal, haven't you heard the saying, when you're in a hole, stop digging?' Irene bade him.

'Yes.' He turned to Kate and smiled with all the charm that had been on view upon their first encounter. She felt her heart miss a beat. He was a strange man, one minute arrogant, almost repellently so, the next compellingly attractive.

Suddenly, all the other men she knew paled into insignificance — and that included Dan — and she found herself wondering how she would have reacted if it had been Fergal who'd kissed her the other evening? 'I'd be very happy to eat any sort of food with you, but if you could hold back on the hemlock and deadly nightshade, I'd be eternally grateful.'

★ ★ ★

Somehow, and entirely unexpectedly, Kate found herself enjoying the evening. Irene, as she already knew, was a joy to spend time with, mainly due to her flashes of acerbic wit and her highly developed sense of humour, and as for Fergal — well, he proved to be every bit as entertaining. He and Kate discovered a shared love of reading and the music of Vivaldi.

'Have you read any of Wilbur Smith's

books?' he asked at one point.

'One or two. Nothing recently.'

'His latest ones are different to the African series. I'll lend you one.'

And they were away, discussing everything from their favourite authors to their favourite food.

Irene sat, eyes narrowed with speculation, listening to their chatter, making no effort to join in.

Kate was genuinely sorry to see them go at the end of the evening. Still, she wasn't alone for long. Ten minutes after they'd left, Dan showed up on her doorstep.

'Just got back from the village,' he said. 'Thought I'd check you were OK. Was that Fergal's car I saw leaving?'

'It was.'

Dan's face darkened. 'What did he want? More of his friends to be fed? Really, that man's got a cheek.'

'No, he's been to dinner.'

If blue eyes could have turned green, Kate was convinced Dan's would have done exactly that.

'With Irene,' she diplomatically added.

'Oh, I see.'

He did look a bit happier at that, but when he went on to ask, 'Fancy a nightcap?'

Kate decided she'd had enough for one evening. Her bed was calling, but apart from that, she suspected that Fergal's company might be a hard act to follow.

'No, sorry, Dan, I'm exhausted.'

'Right. Well, OK then. Maybe another time. You know where I am.'

'Is She In Danger?'

Over the next couple of days, and nights, Kate struggled with her fears, as well as her guilt. She felt especially bad about Irene. She was proving to be such a good and trustworthy friend, it didn't seem right to keep her in the dark about her circumstances. But if she told Irene, she'd really have to tell Dan, and how would they react to such deliberate and on-going deception? Supposing they wanted nothing more to do with her?

She wouldn't be able to bear that. To be shunned by the very people who'd made her feel so welcome in the village. And then, there was Fergal. An attraction she hadn't expected to feel for him had sprung into being during the time they'd spent together and then lingered, her imagination working over-time on the likelihood of something more than mere friendship developing between them.

He'd certainly appeared to enjoy her company, with no sign of his customary aloofness; she'd definitely relished his. So where did that leave her and Dan? How could she be attracted to two men at the same time? Was she really that fickle? Her thoughts whirled chaotically.

In an effort to drive all of those disturbing questions from her mind, she decided to do some work on her front garden for a change. With all her efforts having been concentrated on the rear, the small patch was being steadily over-run by brambles, nettles and bindweed.

Also, the rose that grew next to the honeysuckle was in imminent danger of obliterating, not just the front door, but the entire front of the cottage. It needed pruning — or that's what the gardening book that she'd bought said. Not that Kate had the first idea about pruning.

Still, nothing ventured, nothing gained, she decided, as she carried the stepladder outside — accompanied, as always, by Jess. As it was another hot day, she was clad only in an old T-shirt and a pair of shorts. Gingerly, she climbed to the highest step, where she balanced herself, somewhat precariously, and, with secateurs in hand, set to work.

But the task was nowhere near as simple as the book made it sound, and she was soon perspiring freely. The thorns, particularly vicious due to the rose's overgrown state, insisted on attacking her whenever she moved, as well as attaching themselves to her clothes at every opportunity, leading her to question the wisdom of wearing nothing more than a T-shirt and shorts. One especially nasty one caught her across her cheek. It was as if the plant were seeking to revenge itself upon her for her hard cutting back.

'Right,' she muttered, 'I'm definitely getting rid of you.' She stretched upward, reaching for one particularly long branch, and felt the stepladder begin to wobble beneath her.

'What the blazes are you doing?' an

all too familiar voice demanded.

Kate whirled — a serious mistake she realised too late. The stepladder tilted to the side as one of its legs sank into the soft earth.

'No!' Kate yelled. 'Oh, help!'

'Kate!' the voice responded. 'Watch it!'

Too late. The stepladder tilted even further and Kate began to slowly topple off, straight towards a rather large patch of bramble. Fergal didn't hesitate. He opened the gate and leapt inside — reaching Kate just in time to catch her before she landed in the midst of it. Kate distinctly heard the 'whoosh' of his breath as he took the full weight of her.

'That was your fault,' she muttered. 'I was perfectly OK.'

'You didn't look it to me,' Fergal sharply retaliated. 'Don't you know, you should always make sure a stepladder is firmly grounded?'

'If you hadn't shouted . . . ' She glared up at him, trying to ignore the fact that he was cradling her in his arms, as effortlessly as if she'd been a child. Although, she was pleased to note he was breathing rather heavily. Serves him right, she decided. It was all his fault. 'I'd have been perfectly OK.'

'No, you wouldn't. The ground is too soft here. Sooner or later, you'd have fallen whether I'd been here or not,' he rasped.

'Hmm!' Kate responded. 'I was all right.'

'The ladder was already wobbling before I spoke. What were you doing anyway?'

His voice had lowered as he stared down at her. The intriguing little gold specks that she'd glimpsed the last time they'd met had made their appearance in his eyes.

His face was very near hers now, close enough for his breath to feather her skin. She felt goose bumps break out upon her and she gave a small shiver. In an effort to regain her fast disappearing composure, she spoke sharply. 'I was practising my aerobics! What did it look as if I was doing? I was pruning that spiteful, vicious . . . ' She lifted a hand to her cheek.

'You're hurt,' he said. 'And you're bleeding.'

'I wouldn't be at all surprised. The wretched thing was hell bent on attacking me. Revenge for cutting it back, I shouldn't wonder.' Kate's breathing had almost stopped. 'You can put me down now.' She prayed that only she could hear the tremble of her voice.

'Are you sure?'

Kate nodded, the power of speech seeming to have finally given up the ghost.

For his part, Fergal could only stare at her, his eyes, and whatever emotion they contained, hooded by heavy lids.

'Wh-what's wrong?' she stammered. 'H-have I got dirt on my face?' She could think of no other reason for him to be regarding her so intently.

'No.'

'Then why are you staring?' Kate was gradually recovering her equilibrium and spirit. 'Didn't your mother ever tell you it was rude?'

Fergal unexpectedly grinned at her. Kate's heart performed a double somersault. Whatever had happened to her aversion to handsome men? It had started to fade the evening that he and Irene had come to dinner, that's what had happened, and the final remnants had vanquished a second ago, when she'd found herself, against all expectations, in his arms.

'She did, yes.' Almost in slow motion, he let go of her legs. She stood, making no attempt to move away. Just as Fergal made no attempt to remove his arm from about her waist. There wasn't as much as a millimetre between them. She could feel every muscle of him.

Kate took a deep breath. If she didn't free herself, and it looked as if Fergal was leaving it to her to take the initiative, she was going to do something crazy, like kiss him. Panic-stricken, she pulled away and promptly trod on Jess. The dog yelped. 'Sorry, Jess,' she absently murmured.

Desperate to regain a modicum of self-control, she bluntly demanded, 'Why are you here anyway?'

'Did your mother never tell you that was rude?' He'd deftly turned her own words back upon her. Although, there was a suspicious twitch to his lips — as if he were amusing himself at her expense. And let's face it, it wouldn't be for the first time.

'What?'

'To ask such a question. One should phrase it a little more politely.'

'Oh.' She swung away from that knowing gaze and headed for the house, Jess at her heels. The dog had taken absolutely no notice of Fergal's arrival — which was why Kate hadn't known he was there. She lifted fingers that were trembling still to her cheek; they came away stained with blood. 'In that case,' she sarcastically asked, 'to what do I owe the pleasure of your company?'

'I've brought you the book I promised you.'

She turned back. 'I didn't notice a book.'

'No, I — um, had to cast it to one side in order to catch you.' He was holding it now, she saw. What she also saw was the amusement that was once more tugging at his lips. The insinuation being, she assumed, that she was so heavy that he couldn't accommodate both the book and her.

'Oh, I see.' Her lips tightened in vexation as she headed once more for the house and the kitchen. Once inside, she went straight to the sink. She tugged a piece of kitchen roll from its holder and moistened it under the tap.

'Here, let me,' he said. He placed the book upon the worktop and took the sheet of paper from her. He then cupped her chin with one hand and began to gently wipe the blood away with the other. Kate couldn't look at him, although she was acutely aware of his gaze as he worked, just as she was again of the feathering of his breath upon her skin and the smell of his aftershave.

'Sorry. Am I hurting you?'

'N-no, it's fine — well, just a little.' She had to offer some sort of explanation for her trembling. The last thing she wanted was for him to perceive how deeply she was being affected by his touch.

'There you are then. All done.' And he dropped the bloodstained paper onto the worktop, alongside the book.

'Kate.' The word was so quietly spoken, she almost missed it.

She turned her head and her breath caught in her throat at what she saw written upon his face. In that instant, nerves took over and she blurted out the only thing she could think of. 'Coffee?'

'Uh — no.' Fergal looked bemused by this; bewildered, even.

Oh no, Kate agonised. What had he been going to say? Suddenly, that seemed terribly important. Why hadn't she waited?

He checked his watch. 'Sorry, haven't got the time. Appointments all morning.'

Kate nibbled at her bottom lip. Look

at him. How was he doing that? Staying so cool and unaffected by what had just happened between them. In fact, it was as if he couldn't wait to get away. Maybe he was relieved? That she'd stopped him from speaking out? From saying whatever it was he'd been going to say? Kate sighed.

'In fact,' he went on, 'the first one's in twenty minutes.'

★ ★ ★

Once Fergal had gone, Kate didn't feel like carrying on with her pruning. She did pick up all the roses that she'd cut off though, and arranged them in a vase. Their fragrance filled the room. 'Come on,' she said to Jess, 'we'll have a walk. Just the two of us.'

They were on the point of leaving the house when Bush arrived.

'Thought I'd do a bit more in the garden — is that OK?' he asked.

'Sure. Jess and I are off for a walk by the river. We won't be long.' They passed Dan's house. He was standing in a bedroom window. She waved. Was that the vantage point he used to vet all her visitors? She didn't know whether she liked having her comings and goings monitored quite so closely, even by as good a friend as Dan. It made her feel — well, a bit claustrophobic, she supposed.

Once they reached the river bank, Kate let Jess off her lead. The dog ran ahead, busily poking her nose into every rabbit hole she could find. Kate walked, immersed in her own thoughts.

A full fifteen minutes must have elapsed in this way before she heard the unmistakable sound of a twig cracking beneath someone's foot. She glanced around, there was no-one there. No-one at all. So what, or who, had made the sound?

Nervous all of a sudden, she called Jess back to her. Memories of the other two scares had reared their heads. Having the animal at her side would make her feel fractionally safer. But

Jess, for once, didn't respond. Instead, she stood, perfectly still, nose pointed straight ahead, ears upright, staring at a nearby clump of bushes.

Kate followed her look. A figure moved amongst them; a man's figure. This time there was no doubt.

Just as there was no doubt, in Kate's mind at least, that he'd been watching her.

The cold chill of fear edged along her spine. Another swift glance around told her that she was still completely alone. Normally, there were several people, walking with children or dogs. Today — no-one.

'Come on, Jess, let's go.' The sharpness of her tone ensured that the dog came to her immediately. She snapped the lead onto Jess's collar and began to walk swiftly back the way they'd come, towards the village and what she perceived as safety. The sense of security that she'd always enjoyed in these idyllic surroundings had gone.

Suddenly, every bush, every tree, looked

sinister. Hiding places abounded, in fact. Why had she never noticed that before?

She moved as fast as she could without actually breaking into a run. She had the crazy notion that if she did that, the man would run after her. Whereas, if she appeared to be calm, collected, maybe, just maybe, he'd think twice? Even so, it was a good half a mile back, maybe more. Could she maintain her cool for that long? But she refused to think that way.

It wasn't till they were out of sight of the trees that Kate gave way to the incipient panic and broke into a run. Someone called out from behind her. She didn't stop. If anything, she increased her pace. Her heart thundered madly within her breast, its beat seeming to echo inside her head. She was oblivious to all else; the desperate need to be amongst other people, to be safe, was paramount.

'It's all right, girl,' she panted at last. They'd reached the outskirts of the village. She could see rooftops, and then the rears of the shops, the houses — hear the noise of the ceaseless traffic.

It was as she headed for the first of the buildings, it just happened to be Fergal's house, that she heard the sound of footsteps right behind her. Her heart leapt, it felt as if it were beating in her throat now, so wildly was it palpitating. She whirled round. It was a woman with a dog.

'Hey! Wait for me,' the woman cried. 'I've been trying to catch you up — I called!'

Kate didn't recognise her. She had heard someone call, though. Nervously, she asked, 'Trying to catch me up?'

'Yes. I felt safer with someone else around.'

'You saw him too?' Kate blurted the question out.

'Scared me stiff — I mean, what was he doing? Lurking in the bushes like that.'

'Did you manage to get a look at him?'

'No, 'fraid not. He clearly didn't

want to be seen. That's what struck me as bizarre. People around here are so friendly, usually.'

'Kate!'

For the second time, Kate whirled around, her breathing fast and panicky. It was Fergal. He was standing at the end of his drive, staring at her. What was he doing there? Wasn't he supposed to be at meetings all morning?

He walked towards her and the other woman. 'Are you OK? You look a bit shaken and you're out of breath. It can't still be the tussle with the rose bush, surely?'

It was the unknown woman who took it upon herself to explain. 'We've had a bit of a fright. There was a man . . . ' she pointed back, in the direction from which she and Kate had come, 'back there — hiding — just watching.' She gave a rather theatrical shudder. 'Scary!'

'A man? Where?' Fergal's look sharpened, his mouth tightened into a grim line.

Again, it was the other woman who

told him. Fergal didn't hesitate. He set off along the pathway, his expression still a grim one, his stride long and determined.

'Look, I'll get off,' the stranger told Kate. 'I'm expected back. Will you be all right?'

'Yes. In any case, here comes Fergal.'

He hadn't wasted any time, Kate decided.

'Couldn't see anyone and I had a good look round,' he told her. 'If someone was there, he's gone now. Was it the same man as the other night?'

Kate helplessly shook her head. 'I don't know. I couldn't see him clearly enough either time. He could have been.' Again, she shook her head. 'I just don't know.'

'OK.' He took Kate's arm. 'Come along with me. You look as if you're at the end of your tether. I prescribe a spot of TLC and I know just the person to administer it.'

For an instant, Kate thought he meant himself. He was going to invite her into his home. Her heart soared as she visualised herself in his arms. For a second, the image drove all else from her mind. All the fear, the terror — and she wouldn't have thought that possible. Dear Lord! Whatever was happening to her?

Despite her tumultuous feelings as she visualised herself held close, Fergal was the last man she wanted to be attracted to. Memories of the last time she'd made the mistake of falling for a good looking man resurfaced. She couldn't make the same mistake again; she just couldn't. Despite her growing feelings for him. As she'd already determined, Dan was much more her type. 'Irene,' he said.

Kate thudded back down to reality. Clearly, she had no need to worry about repeating past mistakes, he had no intention of administering the TLC himself. She fought to ignore the pang of disappointment. Fergal wasn't for her. Just remember that, she sternly instructed herself. Put all memories of him holding her aside. Because to dwell on them only ensured misery; the pain of eventual rejection. She refused to go through all that heartache again.

'I'd take you to my place,' he went on. 'but I think Irene's might be better — a woman's touch and all that — and it isn't much further on.'

Irene was appalled when she heard what Kate had to say. 'Do you think it's the same person that was in your garden? My goodness, Kate, it could be a stalker!'

Kate shook her head. 'I don't know what to think.'

And she didn't. Other than the fact that once she'd calmed her emotions, she'd had time to reluctantly reflect that it was something of a coincidence Fergal being around right afterwards. As he'd proved, it would only have taken him seconds to cover the distance from where she'd seen the figure to his driveway.

Yet, for all her distrust of handsome men and their motives, she couldn't believe it had been him. Anyway, he'd have had to have passed her. Unless — part of his garden must back onto the stretch of meadow that ran behind the bushes? He could have returned that way to the house and she wouldn't have seen him, But why would he do something like that? He had no need of money — if that was the motive behind it all? It didn't make sense. None of it did. A small sob worked its way out of her.

'Are you going to report this to the police?' he now demanded.

'Of course she is,' Irene put in.

'What's the point?' Kate miserably argued. 'He'd gone when you went to look, Fergal. Without some evidence to say he was there, and why, there's nothing much the police can do. I told you — I can't give a description of him, I couldn't see him clearly enough.' Just as she hadn't been able to the first time. 'And he didn't threaten me in any way. He was just there — watching.' She shuddered. 'It might not even have been me he was watching. The other woman saw him — it could have been her.'

'After the other night?' he scoffed. 'Unlikely. The two incidents have to be connected. It would be too much of a coincidence for them not to be.'

Kate shivered. His words reinforced her theory that the same person had been behind the previous two incidents: the late night intrusion into her garden, and the anonymous letter. Which would make the likelihood that he was also responsible for this latest scare all the more plausible. All of which, if taken to its logical conclusion, meant that someone was cold-bloodedly targeting her, or, as Irene had suggested, stalking her.

A shaft of pure fear stabbed her. It left her with one vital question. What did whoever it was want? Money? Some of her lottery win? All of her lottery win? That would seem the most obvious reason. Yet, no demands had been made.

'Think, Kate! Is there anyone at all

who might bear you a grudge? Who might want to scare you as some sort of weird revenge?'

'I haven't been here long enough for that, surely?'

'Who's to say? There are some pretty strange characters around nowadays. How about someone from where you were living before?'

That notion hadn't occurred to Kate. If that were true, then it couldn't have been Fergal. But who would do something like this? Sally? Kate had left her her new address, and she had been pretty bitter. Bitter enough to do something like this?

No, Kate didn't think so. And Birmingham was too far away for her simply to pop along and lurk amongst bushes, beneath trees — on the chance of spotting Kate. Or was it? It would only take an hour or so by car. No, Sally would never do such a thing. In any case, it was definitely a man, that much she could be sure of. She decided to change the subject. 'I thought you had meetings all morning? You said you did.' She bit her bottom lip. She sounded accusing.

'Yes, I know,' his smile was a rueful one, 'but my secretary called me on my mobile and told me the first one had been cancelled. So, I was about to come and see if that cup of coffee was still on offer.' He paused, his jaw hardening, his mouth thinning to an implacable line, as her tone obviously got through to him. 'You almost sound as if you're asking me to account for my movements.'

'Fergal,' Irene scoffed, 'don't be so ridiculous. Kate doesn't believe it's you.'

'Don't you, Kate?' A single muscle flexed in his cheek. His eyes had darkened until they were the colour of a wintry sky, and his lips had compressed into a thin line once more. Only this time it wasn't the idea of the unknown watcher who'd provoked the change; this time, it was her, Kate.

'Of course not.' And she didn't, she

really didn't. Fergal was the last man to behave in such an underhand fashion, especially after the way he'd held her earlier; looked at her. How could he have done that if he'd been planning to terrorise her just half-an-hour later? And how would he have known she'd be walking by the river, in any case?

As clearly the watcher had known, otherwise why wait there? She'd made no mention of it to Fergal, hadn't even thought of it while they'd been together. He could have spotted her passing his house, though, a tiny voice suggested, then made his way via his garden to the clump of bushes in time for her to pass by. No, she simply couldn't believe that. Something else occurred to her then. She'd told Bush where she was headed.

Then there was Dan. He'd seen her setting off with Jess. He knew how she loved the riverside. Oh no, she was starting to suspect everyone, even her friends. She was becoming paranoid.

'I was going to ask you out again

— for a meal. However, if you don't trust me,' he shrugged, as if he really didn't care either way, 'there wouldn't be much point.'

'Of course she trusts you.' This was Irene speaking again. 'Here, Kate, your cup of tea, plenty of sugar in it, she's in shock,' she sternly told Fergal. 'She doesn't know what she's saying.'

Kate's hand shook as she took it, the dark tea slopping dangerously near to the top of the cup. Fergal removed it from her grasp and placed it on the table. 'Leave it for a while, till it cools. You don't want to scald yourself into the bargain.'

Eventually, she managed to steady herself sufficiently to drink it. Fergal then said, 'Come on, I'll see you and Jess home.'

So, he did care about her. Otherwise, why would he want to make sure she got home safely?

'No, it's OK, Fergal,' Irene said. 'I'll go with them. You get off to work. I'll probably stay at the cottage for a while, just till Kate's feeling better.'

With Kate struggling to suppress the disappointment that it was Irene and not Fergal with her, they walked back to Bower Cottage. They passed Dan's house, naturally. Kate noticed that all the windows were closed — as if he were out. By the river? She couldn't help wondering.

But he wasn't the only one whose whereabouts were in doubt. When she and Irene reached the cottage, Bush, also, had gone.

Dan Reveals His Feelings

The next morning, Kate decided to give her usual walk by the river a miss. She wanted to be somewhere where there'd be plenty of people around, that was the only way she'd feel safe. She hadn't been back to Box Wood, she realised, since the day of the demonstration, so why not go now? She was curious about the protesters, the eco warriors, and about how they were living. It would also give her the opportunity to find out why Bush hadn't still been in the garden when she'd returned yesterday.

She needed to know, for her own peace of mind, if nothing else. He normally stayed for hours, so something must have happened to send him away early. He didn't talk much about camp life when he was with her, which meant she couldn't even begin to imagine residing on a permanent basis in the branches of trees, but, thank goodness, the protesters didn't mind, otherwise who knows what would have happened to the woodland. It would most likely have been completely felled by now. The village had a lot to thank them for. The least she could do was pay them a visit; show an interest.

So, 'Come on, Jess,' she said, 'let's go.' As she always did, she attached the lead to Jess's collar for the walk along the narrow lane that led from Bower Cottage to the village. She passed Dan's house and for once saw no sign of her neighbour. Which suggested that he must be out, because he was usually there in one window or another.

It was a glorious morning, the sort that made you want to walk for miles. The sun was blazing from an azure sky, its slanting rays making the hedgerows glow emerald, and, in the process, its heat released the scent from the multitude of wild flowers that flourished there.

What made it really perfect was that there was just enough of a breeze to refresh. Kate took a deep breath, relishing the purity of the country air and, for a brief moment, managing to put aside all her worries and fears.

A bird, a skylark, she thought, sang from way on high. She shielded her eyes and peered upwards. Yes, there it was; a minute black speck against the blue. She stood and watched it; it was practically invisible, other than to a really keen eye. The sound of a car engine reached her, disturbing her enjoyment of the scene.

A tinge of anxiety about who the driver might be momentarily made itself felt, and she pulled Jess into the side of the road just as the vehicle rounded the bend in front of her. The driver, obviously seeing her, slowed and pulled to a halt. It was Dan. Relief, mingled with apprehension, swamped her — swiftly followed by anger. This was the dire state of mind to which her persecutor had reduced her; a state of mind that led her to suspect everyone, even her closest friends.

Dan wound down the window. 'Morning. Where are you off to?'

'I thought I'd pay a visit to the camp at Box Wood. See how they're getting on and if they need anything.'

Dan's expression darkened. 'I drove past the other day. It's an awful mess. I wouldn't advise going. Who knows what you'll catch?'

'I'm good and healthy and have a very strong immune system, so I doubt I'll catch anything. But thanks for the warning.'

'No, really, Kate. It looks positively unhygienic.'

'I'll be OK, Dan. Don't worry.'

'Be it on your own head then,' he said, somewhat sharply.

'I'll talk to you later.'

'Fine.'

'Got your mobile phone on you?'

'Of course.' She never went anywhere without it.

'If you need me, just ring.'

'I'm sure I won't.' Goodness! Anyone would think she was planning to venture into a den of criminals.

'Well, I'm not. In my opinion, anyone who chooses to permanently live up a tree must need his, or her, head examining. So, who knows what they'd be capable of?'

She just hoped he wasn't right — at least as far as Bush was concerned, considering the amount of time he spent in her garden. Nonetheless, she kept her tone light. She didn't want to encourage his theory that she could be in some sort of danger. He was already protective enough of her. 'Oh Dan, they're harmless. They're just some environmentally conscious people. Their only fault is to be idealistic.'

'Huh!' He pressed his foot on his accelerator, noisily racing the engine. 'If that's what you want to call it. I'd call it fanatical.'

'Well, without them there, Box Wood would most likely have disappeared by now. Is that what you want?'

'Maybe it would and maybe it wouldn't have,' and with those abrupt words he was gone.

* * *

But when Kate got to Box Wood, she realised that Dan had grossly exaggerated.

Oh, it was untidy, sure enough, but what camp wasn't? Of the unhygienic conditions that he had warned her about, she could see very little evidence. There were a couple of heaps of rubbish, but nothing too bad. In fact, she was astonished at what they'd achieved in a relatively short time. There were lots of tree houses, with rope ladders for getting up to them.

A couple of fires burned in specially dug out pits with pots suspended over them, cooking pots if the appetising aromas of stewing meat and vegetables reaching Kate's nostrils were anything to go by. Banners also hung around the perimeter of the site, with the words

HANDS OFF OUR WOODS painted on them in giant red letters.

'Hey, Kate.'

Kate swung round. It was Bush, hailing her from the branches of a huge old oak tree. He was standing on a wooden platform, over which he had suspended a large tarpaulin for shelter. She waved.

'Hang on, I'll come down,' he called.

He quickly and expertly slid down the rope, something he'd clearly done many times before, and stood in front of Kate, a broad and delighted grin wreathing his features.

'This is a surprise,' he exclaimed. 'Nothing wrong, is there?' He considered her, his head to one side, the grin extinguished now by a frown of concern.

'No, I just thought — well, I haven't visited yet and frankly, I was curious.'

'So . . . ' he waved an arm, indicating the activity all around them, 'what do you think?'

'It's great, astonishing, actually. You've

worked miracles — all of you. It's a second village, a treetop village. I love it.' And she clasped her hands in front of her, chuckling with delight as she did so. She glanced around. 'I hadn't realised there were so many of you.'

People were moving around, completely at ease, both high in the trees and on the ground. A quick head count came up with a rough estimate of thirty or forty. 'Um, I wondered if you were OK, actually. Only you'd gone by the time I got home yesterday.'

'Yeah.' He lifted a hand to his forehead, where she noticed for the first time a faint bruising. 'I managed to bang it and give myself a headache, so I thought I'd give it a rest for a day or two,' and he grinned. Clearly, it wasn't bothering him unduly now.

'Bush, I'm sorry. It's my fault. I shouldn't have agreed to you helping me.' It did seem to let him off the hook, however, with regards to whoever it had been watching her by the river. Unless he'd deliberately inflicted the bruise to throw her off the scent? Oh Lord! There she went again. Suspecting a friend; a friend, moreover, who'd been unstinting in his help. She should be ashamed.

'Don't be silly. I offered, and it's not that bad.'

'Well, if you say so.'

'Hey, while you're here, you ought to meet a few of the crowd.'

'I'd love to.' And she really would. Then, providing they were just ordinary people, and not a bunch of predatory stalkers, which was highly unlikely, she could confidently assure Dan that they meant her no harm.

★　★　★

It was a full hour later that Kate left the camp site, fully reassured, as she had expected to be, by the protesters eager welcome of her and Bush's genuine warmth towards her. Dan had had no need to be worried about her. All right, so some of them dressed a bit strangely, but, all in all, they were just normal young people. Whatever normal was these days?

She eventually said goodbye to them and promised to visit again. Next time, she vowed, she'd take them some home-cooked food. She was sure they'd welcome that, because there must be certain things you simply couldn't cook on an open fire.

She left Box Wood with a last wave to Bush, and continued her walk along the lane that bordered it. Gradually, the morning had turned from the initially pleasantly warm one into an oppressively hot and humid one. Even the sky, she saw, had gone from a clear blue to a strange, yellowy grey. Maybe she'd better head for home before the rain that the heavy sky seemed to threaten arrived.

She had just turned into her own lane when she felt the first heavy drops and heard the first peal of thunder.

'Oh no,' she groaned. She still had quite a way to go and she'd always hated thunder. As a child it had raised the terrifying spectre of a giant furiously striding around the heavens above her. The thunder had been his menacing growl. Jess began to whimper as Kate fastened the lead to her collar once more. 'Come on, girl, I think we'd better make a run for home, otherwise we're going to get awfully wet.'

Her decision was taken too late, however. Within a matter of seconds, the few drops had transformed themselves into a veritable deluge and her thin blouse and jeans were sodden. By the time they reached the house, she and Jess were literally dripping. She opened the front door with considerable relief, and almost trod on the envelope lying just inside on the floor.

Ignoring it for the moment, she led a very sorry and bedraggled Jess into the kitchen, where she briskly rubbed her down with the towel that she kept specifically for that purpose. It wasn't until she'd stripped off her own wet clothes and had a tepid shower that she went back downstairs and retrieved the envelope.

It was addressed simply, the single word, KATE, scrawled across the envelope. A shudder of apprehension went through her. It looked like the handwriting that had been on the first anonymous letter. With a sinking feeling in the pit of her stomach, she ripped it open. The single sheet of paper inside was covered in crudely printed capitals.

She read: WHY DON'T YOU BE HONEST? I KNOW WHO YOU ARE. WHY DON'T YOU LIVE LIKE THE MILLIONAIRESS THAT YOU ARE? HAVE YOU SPENT ALL THE MONEY? OR ARE YOU JUST TOO MEAN TO SHARE IT? WELL, I'LL BE WATCH-ING YOU. JUST REMEMBER THAT.

And that was it. Once again, no perceptible threat, other than for the words I'LL BE WATCHING YOU. Could that be considered a threat? She didn't know. Also, there was still no actual demand for money: Kate was perplexed. What was the point? To frighten her? Because it was working. The tears stung her eyes. Why was this happening to her? Who hated her enough to torment her in such a way?

It had to be someone who knew her. Who knew the way she was living, simply and without ostentation. Who also knew what time she went walking each day. Because the letter must have been delivered in the last couple of hours, when the writer knew she would be out. He, or she, wouldn't want to risk being seen. It certainly hadn't been on the floor when she left the house because she would have had to walk over it to get through the door and she'd have seen it.

The worst thing about all of this was that she couldn't really talk about the letters to any of her friends. If she did that, she'd have to tell them the truth about her lottery win, otherwise how would she explain what it said? And then, the full depths of her deceit would be revealed. Unless, of course, as she'd wondered a couple of times already, the culprit was one of those friends. They'd all had the time — and the opportunity

She covered her face with both hands. That would be the worst outcome of all; an outcome that she really didn't want to consider. But the plain truth was that Dan had known she was going to be out for some time, Fergal probably knew her daily routine by now, and Bush would have had more than enough time to reach the cottage between her leaving Box Wood and arriving home again.

★　★　★

In a desperate attempt to drive everything that was happening from her mind and rid herself of the unwanted suspicions, Kate returned to her pruning. She had to — no, needed to — carry on as normal. For the sake of her own sanity. Not wanting a repeat of yesterday's performance, she made sure that the step ladder was firmly grounded.

Not that she believed Fergal would put in an appearance again in the wake of her ill-disguised suspicion of him.

Although, he had seemed to get over his anger — if his offer to see her home had been anything to go by. The thought comforted her, somewhat, as well as bolstering her faith that the culprit wasn't him.

It was the gate squealing behind her that alerted her to someone's arrival. She couldn't help it, her heart leapt. Could it be Fergal? Jess whimpered, making her turn her head. Dan was staring up at her.

'What's this I hear about someone spying on you again?' He must mean the incident by the river. Amazingly, the arrival of the second letter had driven it from her mind, for a while at least. He looked angry, as if it was her fault that she'd been watched.

'Who told you that?'

'It's all round the village. Some other woman saw him too, apparently. She says you were definitely the target.'

So, the woman had known who she was, even if Kate hadn't known her. 'Why does she think that?'

'It was you he was watching.'

Kate didn't respond.

'So, is it true?'

'Yes.'

'Why didn't you come to me afterwards? For goodness sake, Kate, I've said it enough times now. What more do I have to do to convince you I have your best interests at heart? That I'm here for you — always.'

'It wouldn't have been any good coming to you, Dan, you were out.' She watched closely for any sign, any indication, a reddening of the skin, a look of guilt, that it could have been him by the river. There wasn't one. He just looked concerned for her.

She was relieved, as relieved as she had been by her reasoning that the watcher couldn't have been Fergal. And she really didn't want to believe the stalker was Dan, not living as close to her as he did. That would be freaky. Of course, she also didn't want to believe it was Bush either.

'Oh, right That must have been when

I popped out for a newspaper. But, you could have waited. I wasn't gone long.'

'There was no need. I bumped into Fergal afterwards. He took me to Irene's. She administered tea and sympathy perfectly adequately.'

'I can't believe it! I actually saw you leaving. I could have gone with you. I will in future.'

Kate gingerly descended from her perch. 'No, you won't, Dan.'

'How much do you bet it was one of that rabble in the camp?' He stopped talking and eyed her guardedly. 'Were you OK this morning? I should have come with you.'

'No, you shouldn't have. I don't know what this person's motives are, but I refuse to be intimidated or stopped from doing what I want to.'

Before she could finish speaking, however, Dan caught hold of her by the arms. 'Listen, Kate. Let me take care of you.'

'I don't need anyone to take care of me, Dan,' she began. But was that true?

she demanded of herself. She'd have been glad of someone with her when any one of the incidents had occurred.

Dan's eyes had darkened at her words. He clearly didn't believe her. 'Are you sure about that?'

'Y-yes.' Her voice trembled, belying the sentiment she had just voiced. She could feel his hands tightening upon her. He did seem genuinely upset by it all. Kate stared up at him, her eyes liquid and gleaming. Maybe she should confide in him?

'Blast,' he groaned. 'You must know how I feel about you.' He pulled her closer. He made to kiss her.

But Kate wasn't in any mood for that. Suddenly, it wasn't Dan that she wanted holding her. It was — oh no, she silently groaned, she couldn't be that foolish — could she? She moved her head sideways. 'Dan, no.'

'I'm falling in love with you,' he muttered. 'You must know.' He lifted a hand to cup her chin, trying to turn her face to his. Kate resisted.

'And you're driving me to distraction. It's time to settle things,' he muttered.

'Dan, no. I don't think so.' All desire to confide in him had vanished, extinguished by his controlling nature. She didn't need this, not now, not in the immediate aftermath of the arrival of a second letter. Forgetting she didn't want to offend him, or hurt his feelings, she pushed him away. What had happened to the concern she'd thought she'd seen?

'What on earth is going on here?'

The grating tones were Fergal's. 'Peters? Are you stark, staring mad? Didn't you hear her? Leave her alone.'

Fergal strode through the open gate and caught hold of Dan by the back of his shirt, literally yanking him away from Kate.

'Mind your own business, Cameron.' Dan looked furious. His face was puce with outrage. 'She doesn't need you.'

'That's debatable,' Fergal replied angrily. 'And it's certainly not how it looked to me. Now . . . ' Keeping hold

178

of Dan, he began to steer him across the garden. Which didn't prove too difficult a task as Fergal was at least six feet one or two to Dan's five feet eight or so.

Nonetheless, Dan managed to break free of his grip and whirled, to lash out at him with a clenched fist, saying, 'Take your hands off me — you — you!' Fergal neatly sidestepped the blow.

Dan tried again, and missed again. Furious, he began to flail, his arms windmilling in all directions. A steely-eyed Fergal muttered, 'Right, if that's how you want to play it,' and hit him squarely on the jaw, not hard, just firmly enough to render Dan motionless and silent.

'That's better,' Fergal growled. 'Now, Kate said no. She doesn't want you near her, so go home and don't come back. Understand?'

Dan glared at Fergal before turning his gaze upon Kate. 'Is that what you want, Kate?'

'Dan,' she pleaded. 'Please, just go.'

Dan stared at her, his expression one of outraged disbelief. 'After all I've done?'

'Dan, not now.' She mustered a weak smile. 'We'll talk later, OK?' She felt bad about this. Up till the moment he'd tried to kiss her, he'd only been trying to protect her, she was sure, from what he viewed as some sort of threat to her well-being. But something had changed in those last minutes, and not just in her.

From being concerned about her welfare, Dan had become threatening. What if Fergal hadn't turned up? Well, she didn't want to think about what might have happened.

One thing she did think, however, was that it was time to cool things between her and Dan. He was starting to presume too much; to think he had some sort of right of possession over her. He had to be shown that he didn't; no-one did. Nonetheless, she watched in abject horror as Dan extricated himself from Fergal's grip and stormed off, back towards his house.

Kate's Troubles Get Worse

'Are you okay?' Fergal asked her. He was watching her closely, his eyes narrowed, their gaze penetrating. 'Did he scare you?'

Kate shook her head. 'Not really. I'm fine.' Her impression that he had decided to disregard her implied accusation of the day before that the stalker might be him was confirmed. The cold look that had been in his eyes then had now been replaced by deep concern — and something else. Something unfathomable. Whatever it was, it made her feel safe — cherished; protected.

'Has he tried anything like that before?'

'N-no.' He had, of course, outside of The Feathers, but his kiss had been different then, no indication of force, and he'd halted things straight away. However, she wasn't about to tell Fergal that. It was no-one's business but hers — and Dan's.

'Let's go inside,' he said. 'You look very shaken.'

'I'm OK.' Kate just wanted to be left alone if the truth were told. She felt as if she were being torn apart by completely opposing forces. She wanted time to come to terms with what she'd just experienced and what she'd subsequently learnt from that experience. 'Um, did you come for something?'

'Yes, I came to see if you were OK after yesterday's little incident. You do get yourself into some scrapes, don't you?' Kate didn't respond. 'Anyway, I also came to let you know that the proposed road has been shelved — permanently. Something to do with lack of funds, or so the powers that be say. I think they've simply decided there's too much opposition.'

'Oh, that's good. Does that mean the

eco-warriors will be leaving?'

'I should think so. So, what I also was going to say was that with Bush gone, if you wanted any help in the garden?'

'Oh, that is kind, but it's almost finished.' She didn't know how she'd cope with Fergal around here on a regular basis. How she would conceal her growing feelings for him? Which, as she really didn't have a clue as to how he felt about her, could be a mite embarrassing. She should have let him say whatever it was he'd intended the day before. Even if it hadn't been what she'd wanted to hear, at least she'd have known where she stood.

★   ★   ★

Kate's next visitor was Bush and he did, indeed, tell her he was leaving the village. 'We're off to another site. Another unwanted and completely unnecessary road that will, if built, destroy an invaluable piece of our countryside.'

She'd miss him, Kate realised, even if she hadn't been able to help wondering if he could be the one watching her. Although, if the stalking stopped? It would be the proof she needed that it had been him. Her nightmare would be over.

But it wasn't to be.

The following day, while Kate was preparing an omelette for her lunch, the phone rang. She lifted the receiver to be greeted by silence.

'Hello. Who's there?'

When she still received no answer, she assumed it was a wrong number and hung up. Exactly one hour later, the procedure was repeated. This time, she rang 1471, only to be told that the caller had withheld the number.

By the time it had happened half a dozen times, she was convinced that her theory was the correct one. Someone was systematically and deliberately terrorising her. Presumably, so that when they made their eventual demand for money she'd readily pay just to stop what was happening. It was the only reason she could think of. And, contrary to what she'd suspected previously, it didn't necessarily have to be someone she knew personally. It could be anyone. She didn't know whether that made her feel better or not.

Eventually, as suddenly as it had started, it stopped and the evening passed with no disturbances of any sort. Until the early hours of the morning.

This time Kate was ready. 'I don't know who you are or why you're doing this, but if it doesn't stop, I'm calling the police. I'm sure they have the means of tracing your phone number!'

The next day Irene called. Kate was completing the planting round the pool that Bush had dug out and then filled with water for her, hard work, she'd found, being the only thing that kept her mind off her steadily intensifying troubles.

'Kate? Did you know your front door was on the latch?'

Kate was so startled she dropped the

plant pot she was holding. Normally, the squealing of the gate warned her of someone's arrival. And if not that, then Jess certainly did. However, Jess was inside, asleep.

'Why,' Irene exclaimed, 'whatever's wrong? You're as white as a sheet.'

'Oh, Irene, you took me by surprise but, oh am I glad to see you,' and she proceeded to tell her about the phone calls.

Irene looked almost as distressed as Kate was. ''And you left your door unlocked? I could have been anyone.'

'I know. I can't even remember unlocking the door. I'm in such a state to tell the truth, I don't know what I am doing.' She gave a shaky laugh as tears stung her eyes and then began to overflow. She was shaking uncontrollably. So much so, that she was afraid to bend and pick up the dropped pot in case she fell completely over.

'Kate, my dear,' Irene crossed to her and put an arm about her shoulders. 'Come on. I'll put the kettle on.'

'Yes, please.' Kate sniffed, wiping her eyes. 'Sorry. I don't know what came over me then.'

'I do,' Irene retorted, 'it's called plain, old-fashioned fear. You've reported the phone calls to the police, I presume?'

'No.'

'Oh, Kate, why ever not?' She sounded exasperated.

'What's the point? What can they do? Oh Irene, whoever's doing this to me is still walking round free as air while I'm . . . '

'Are you sure it's the same person?'

'It has to be. There can't be more than one individual cruel enough to be tormenting me like this?'

'I think you should come and stay with me for a while.'

Kate was sorely tempted. 'What would that solve? Whoever it is would simply wait for me to return home, I'm sure, which I'd have to do eventually.'

'Are you positive you know of no reason why anyone should be doing these things?'

Kate looked away from Irene's enquiring gaze. 'No, I can't think of anything.' How could she tell Irene the truth now? As she'd already concluded, she was caught in a trap, and what was worse, it was a trap entirely of her own making. She should have been open and above board right from the start. She should have let people make up their own minds about her.

To Kate's relief, there were no more phone calls. That didn't stop her wondering, though, whether she should move back to Birmingham. The anonymity of a large city was beginning to look more and more appealing. 'What shall we do, Jess?' she asked her pet at one point. 'Shall we move?'

The dog whined, rubbing herself against Kate's leg. Kate smiled and ruffled the dog's head. 'You're right, we stay.'

The Strain Begins
To Show

It wasn't long before she was questioning the wisdom of that decision: the very next night, in fact.

Kate was on the point of falling asleep when the sound of Jess padding about the bedroom, whining as she did so, had her sitting up again.

'What is it, Jess?' she nervously asked.

The dog gave a sharp bark and jumped up at the window.

'Is someone out there?' Kate got out of bed, somewhat shakily it had to be said. Surely there couldn't be an intruder in the back garden?

She crossed to the window and pulled back a curtain, just far enough for her to peer into the darkness outside.

'Oh, no!' She leapt back in horror, almost treading on Jess as she did so.

The dog whimpered and leapt out of the way. 'Ssh, quiet, Jess,' she whispered.

There was someone out there. Someone clothed all in black, head covered in a hood, and they were in the process of pulling up all the plants that Kate had so laboriously planted a couple of days before and tossing them onto a growing heap at his side.

The anger ripped through Kate, in an instant replacing the fear that had so afflicted her just seconds ago. Swiftly, she pulled on a sweater and trousers. She had to stop him was all she could think. No way was all her work going to be for nothing.

Not giving a thought to her own safety, she ran down the stairs, Jess at her heels, through the kitchen and out into the garden — just in time to see the figure running down the side path of the house towards the front gate and escape.

'Stop!' she shouted. 'Who are you? What do you want with me?' But she was too late. He was gone.

She ran to the gate, which was swinging open, and stood in the lane, looking wildly in each direction, frantically searching for any clue as to the identity of the intruder. It was no good, he'd gone. For it had been a man again, she was positive about that. The figure had looked too solid, too bulky for a woman. Even in the darkness she'd been able to see that.

Slowly now, she walked back into her garden and there, stood, surveying the wreckage. It had taken her several hours to accomplish, but now almost every plant that she had so lovingly set in the ground had been torn from the soil. Some, she saw upon closer inspection, were too badly damaged to replant; quite a few, however, looked intact.

Fetching her trowel and a spade from the small shed that now stood against a hedge, she doggedly began to work. Tears filled her eyes, blurring her view of what she was doing, but she didn't care. Blindly, she carried on until every plant that was worth salvaging was once more in its rightful place.

The moon, which had been full, fortunately, enabling her to see what she was doing, had disappeared and dawn was tinting the sky gold as she finished. Wearily, she replaced her tools in the shed and went inside.

'Oh, Jess,' she sighed, 'what am I going to do?'

The dog pushed her nose gently into Kate's palm and whimpered, her tail going from side to side like a piston. The gentle animal was offering what comfort she could.

'If I move back to Birmingham, will whoever it is doing this to me just follow? If only he'd say what it is he wants. If it's money, I'll gladly pay just to get some peace of mind.' Although she knew that would be wrong. She didn't care about that, however. All she wanted was to be left alone. 'Come on, let's go and get some sleep. He won't come back now, not in the daylight.'

But supposing he came back that night? And repeated the performance? What then?

She was too exhausted to think about that for the moment and the second her head touched the pillow she was asleep. It was a fitful sleep, filled with disturbing images and dreams. Wild animals were snarling at the doors and windows, trying to get inside. She could hear their claws tearing at the wood of the window frames. She tossed and turned relentlessly, until eventually she did lapse into a heavy and dreamless slumber.

It was the smashing of glass that awoke her and then the pronounced racing of a car engine. She sprang upright in her bed, not sure if she'd really heard it or if she'd simply been dreaming again. She listened intently, but all was silent.

'Jess?' Where was the dog? She'd been at Kate's side as Kate fell asleep. Oh no! What now? Suddenly, she heard Jess barking. 'Jess?' she repeated, clambering from the bed and glancing at the clock as she did so. It was ten o'clock.

She ran down the stairs. Her feet were bare and she was hardly awake. Jess's barking was coming from the sitting room. Kate ran in and then stopped abruptly, unable to credit what it was she was looking at.

Jess was standing in the centre of a carpet of broken glass, in the midst of which sat a brick. Clearly, someone had heaved it through the window, shattering the large, middle pane completely, leaving the two on either side intact, and then driven off.

Kate sank onto the settee, mindful of possible injury to her bare feet. She couldn't believe it. Who was persecuting her like this? How could anyone be so cruel? So callous? Someone who wanted a share of her millions? Sally's name again sprang unbidden into her head. She'd wanted a share, but her stalker was definitely a man, not a woman.

Yes, logic whispered, but Sally could have got someone else to do her dirty work for her? Someone whom Kate wouldn't recognise. She dropped her face into her hands. She couldn't believe it, not of her one-time best friend. Maybe if she went to see Sally, offered her some money; maybe that would stop it?

She'd wanted to give her some at the time of the win, but Sally had persisted with her declaration that she didn't want any. Maybe time had changed her mind? It was the only answer Kate could come up with. She'd been so careful to keep her identity a secret here in the village. Surely no-one could have uncovered the truth?

A small sob worked its way up her throat. She suppressed it. She had to stay calm. She also had to make sure that Jess negotiated her way through the shards of broken glass unscathed.

'Jess. Come here, darling. Careful now.' All she could think then was of the possible danger to her pet. A shard of glass in her paw could do untold damage. 'Come on,' she gently urged.

Jess picked her way through the detritus that lay all around her and reached Kate with no evidence of any injury. Kate grabbed hold of her and pulled her close, burying her face in the animal's fur as she wept, silently and despairingly.

What was she going to do? Ring the police? But supposing it was Sally?

It was then, as if her thoughts had induced it, that the phone rang. She lifted her head and stared at it, transfixed with dread. Was it the silent caller? Ringing to evaluate the effect his persecution was having upon her? Slowly, wearily, she leant over and lifted the receiver. She didn't speak. All she could hear was the sound of someone breathing on the other end. She stiffened.

'Kate? Are you there?'

It was Fergal. She let out the breath she hadn't even realised she was holding, and unable to help herself, she began to weep.

'Kate?' Fergal's tone had sharpened. 'Kate — OK. Hold on. I'll be there in two minutes.'

And he was. He must have moved like the wind. She heard the screech of his car brakes as he literally slammed them on and skidded to a halt. Kate opened the door and led him into the sitting room. She pointed to the broken window, and the shards of glass lying all around.

'My word! What happened?'

She told him. She also told him about the plants being uprooted in the garden.

'And you actually saw the person doing it?'

'Yes.'

Fergal looked horrified. 'And yet you went out there?'

She nodded.

'This — on top of the phone calls — oh, yes, Irene told me. You do realise what could have happened, don't you? He could have attacked you. Never mind the blasted plants, they're replaceable.'

'I didn't think of that. I was so angry — after all my hard work, I-I didn't want him to win.' Tears once more sprang to her eyes. She dashed them away, furious with her display of weakness.

Fergal stared at her. 'Come here,' was all he said, opening his arms.

Blindly, Kate stepped into them. He enfolded her in his embrace. 'You're a very brave woman, but, I have to say, also an extremely foolish one.'

'I know.' Kate gave a tearful grin, blinking up at him through the moisture that lingered in her eyes. Once again, she felt safe, protected.

His eyes narrowed until they were no more than slits as he looked down at her; his mouth tightened. A muscle flexed in his jaw.

He was angry with her, despite his gentle words, was all she could think. She tried to pull away but his grip held her firmly in place. Her eyes widened as she felt a spasmodic flare of alarm. Had she, in her foolishness, actually allowed

198

her tormentor to come into her home? And if so, what would he do now?

But her fear was baseless. For he gently moved forward and gave her a tender kiss. 'Oh, Kate,' he murmured, and all her fears were put to one side as she admitted what she'd suspected for a while now — she was dangerously attracted to Fergal Cameron.

The man she couldn't be a hundred per cent sure wasn't behind each and every incident that had befallen her.

Dear Lord! What on earth was she doing? She wrenched herself free and stood, her arms wrapped around herself, in a desperate attempt to stop the trembling that was afflicting every single part of her.

'Kate?' He smiled quizzically, shakily, even.

'S-sorry,' she stammered. 'I don't know what happened.'

His smiled vanished, and a strange expression flared in the depths of his dark eyes. An eyebrow lifted. 'It did take you several moments to decide you didn't want me kissing you. That suggests to me . . . '

'Whatever it suggested to you, all it meant was that-that I-I was upset. I didn't know what I was doing.'

He said nothing, seemingly quite content to allow her to go blundering on. Then, 'Kate,' the single word was gently said. The unfathomable expression had gone, leaving in its wake a compassion so deep it practically reduced Kate to a shivering jelly, 'there's nothing wrong with a man and a woman falling in love.'

'No, I know, but . . . '

'But?'

The eyebrow lifted again, just as the first signs of amusement appeared upon his face.

'Well, emotions become unduly exaggerated, even, in times of distress. They shouldn't be taken at face value.'

'I see.' The amusement had vanished. Instead, the planes of his face looked as if they had been chiselled out of solid granite. 'Well, to get back to the crucial

question, have you phoned the police?'
His tone was as glacial as his eyes had
become. They reminded Kate of the
photographs she'd seen of the frozen
wastes of Antarctica.

'N-no.'

'Well, don't you think you'd better?'

'I don't see the point. What can they
do? Someone pulled up my plants and
heaved a brick through my window. I
have no idea who it was and neither will
they. They haven't exactly left a calling
card.'

'You don't know what they've left.
There could be fingerprints.'

'What? On the brick? I wouldn't
think so.'

'You should still report it. For an
insurance claim, if nothing else. So, will
you do that or would you like me to?'

'No. I'll do it.' The less she asked of
this cold-eyed, hatchet-faced individual
the better. That way, she wouldn't have
any need to feel in any way indebted to
him.

'Fine. I'll do something about the

broken window — just temporarily. I know a very good man who'll come and do a full replacement within the hour of you calling him. Leave the glass where it is — and the brick.' His tone was one of sarcasm now. 'Regardless of your conviction that it won't provide any clues as to the person who threw it, the police will want to examine it and do their forensics.'

So that's what they did. Kate spoke to someone at the police station, they didn't sound very interested, although, they did promise to send someone round. Kate didn't hold out much hope of that, but she did leave all the evidence — or what evidence there was — in place. It was too late for the plants. She'd already replaced them in the ground.

Fergal, as he'd promised, did a temporary repair on the window, his demeanour throughout unapproachable. Kate bit at her lip. She'd offended him, but she hadn't been able to help herself. How could she kiss a man she didn't fully trust? A man with whom, moreover, she'd been less than honest. She was in the same situation with him as the one she was in with Dan. She'd deceived them both.

How could she begin a relationship with either of them? Even in the event of discovering that they had had no part in any of the incidents?

Fergal finally left with a curt goodbye and an instruction to call him if anything else should happen. He did soften sufficiently at the last minute to say, with what Kate decided was a deliberately provocative smile, 'I promise not to kiss you again.'

Even so, Kate couldn't for the life of her imagine ringing him for help — not after what had just taken place between them. He clearly hadn't believed her when she'd told him her response had been solely due to stress. He knew she was attracted to him.

Two hours later, the glazier arrived — with Dan only minutes behind him.

Kate Gets An Invitation

'What's going on?' was Dan's first question, to be almost immediately followed by, 'Good Lord! What happened?' as he noticed the boarded up window.

'Someone threw a brick through it.'

Dan's face paled. 'When?'

'This morning — at ten o'clock.'

'In broad daylight? Did you see who it was? Have you rung the police?' His initial expression of alarm transformed itself into one of deep anxiety.

In the light of that, she decided not to mention the intruder in the garden and the uprooted plants. He'd probably have a seizure if he heard about that as well. 'Yes, it was in broad daylight and no, I didn't see who it was. All I heard was the sound of a car engine racing away. I have rung the police and they came round about an hour ago.'

'What did they say?'

'Not much.' She shrugged.

She hadn't expected anything else really. After all, what could they say? She'd seen nothing, heard nothing until the glass smashed. She hadn't even caught a glimpse of the getaway car — if that's what it had been. She had given a description of the intruder, but as his face had been completely hidden by his hood, she suspected it hadn't been much use.

'They took the brick away for examination for fingerprints.' They'd also inspected the garden where the plants had been pulled up and then replanted. They hadn't had much to say about that either. There were lots of footprints but they'd been mainly hers, she suspected. Their expressions had implied that, solely due to her contamination of the crime scene, there wasn't a lot they could do.

She shrugged again. She didn't expect any results from their examination of the brick, either. Whoever the perpetrator had been, he, or she, would almost certainly have taken the precaution of wearing gloves. And would they have left prints on something as rough textured as a brick in any case? She didn't know.

'Why didn't you ring me? I'd have come straight round. You must have been terrified.' He took a step towards her. Kate quickly backed away.

He saw it, of course. How could he not have done? He stopped, in mid-stride. 'Look, Kate,' his expression was one of shame, 'the reason I came is to — to apologise. My behaviour was disgraceful, you know, kissing you. Things got out of hand.' His face reddened. 'I didn't mean it to, but I couldn't help myself. Sorry.' His smile was one of abject apology. 'Please say you forgive me.'

'Well,' Kate felt a pang of sympathy for him. Even so, she ignored the hand he held out. He instantly withdrew it, 'we all do things now and then that we regret.'

'I know, but I shouldn't have. Anyway, once again, I'm sorry. And . . . ' he grimaced ruefully, 'you don't need to be nervous of me. I'd never do anything to hurt you in any way.'

'I'm not nervous, Dan, not really. I'm simply upset. Anyway,' she heedlessly rushed on, 'Fergal came round and . . . '

'Fergal!' Even darker colour stained his cheeks now. 'You phoned him? When I'm just next door?'

'I didn't phone him.' Although, what business it was of his who she phoned, she didn't know. Vexation stabbed her.

As she'd thought more than once lately, Dan was growing altogether too possessive of her. She was a free agent. She could ring who she wanted. 'He just happened to ring right after — and — and I was upset so he came round.' Although, why she was explaining all of this she didn't really know.

'What did he want?' He spoke curtly.

What was it between him and Fergal? What had happened to cause this hostility that they invariably displayed towards each other? Look at the other day. They'd actually come to blows. 'I-I just told you, I was upset.' She'd already told him that once.

'No, no.' He shook his head impatiently. 'Why did he ring?'

'Do you know, I didn't ask. I never thought.' That was strange. Why had he rung? He never did say and she'd been too upset to ask him. All she'd been bothered about was the broken window and the fact that someone had been in the garden in the dead of night; someone intent on wreaking havoc. Still, it couldn't have been that important or he'd have said, wouldn't he? Unless, of course, the breath stilled in her throat at the mere notion, the perpetrator had been him and he was phoning to find out what her reaction to the two incidents had been?

For all his faults, and he had many, she simply couldn't believe Fergal capable of such devious behaviour. And look how tender he'd been with her. Would he have acted in such a manner if it had been him behind it all? And what would have been his motive? Not money, surely? He looked to have plenty of his own. I mean, just look at that house. It must be worth a million or two. No, Fergal wasn't short of money.

'Kate, Kate,' he sounded exasperated now, 'I've told you, ring me when you're worried. I'm much nearer than Fergal.'

'I know, but Fergal was here in two minutes.'

'I bet he was,' Dan muttered. 'I could have been here in two seconds.'

Kate didn't respond to that. She was too weary to argue if the truth was known. She'd barely slept.

Eventually Dan left, after extracting a promise from her that if anything untoward happened she'd ring him at once.

'That's it, all done, Miss,' the glazier said.

And that was that, she was alone once again. She yawned and headed for the sofa. A couple of hours sleep, that's what she needed. She arranged the cushions into a pillow, made sure all the doors were locked, and lay down. She'd just started to drift off when the phone rang. She groaned. Who on earth could that be? Irene? Fergal had probably told her what had happened. She reached for the receiver. 'Hello?'

'Kate, it's me, Irene. Fergal told me what's happened. Are you all right?'

'Yes, I-I'm fine.'

'You don't sound it. I'm coming round.'

'No, really there's no need.'

'Yes, yes, there is. You sound decidedly shaky. It'll only take me twenty minutes or so to walk there.'

'No, Irene, really. I'm OK. And it will take at least half an hour.'

'No arguments. I need some fresh air and a walk will do me good.'

'OK, in that case, I'll come and collect you.'

'Absolutely not.' And she hung up.

*   *   *

Sure enough, in just over the half hour that Kate had predicted, the doorbell chimed and Kate opened the door to see the old lady standing there. Immediately, what she had sworn to herself wouldn't happen, happened. The tears welled and she started to quietly weep. 'Oh, Irene, I'm sorry.'

'Don't be. Tears can be a restorative at times like these.' Irene strode inside and swept Kate into her arms. Kate clung to her and allowed the tears to fall freely.

'Now, you can't be on your own, not in this state. Come and stay with me, just for a few days.'

'I can't,' Kate wailed. 'What if something else happens and I'm not here to stop it?'

'I knew you'd say that. In which case, I'll come and stay with you.'

Kate stared at her friend. 'Would you, would you really?'

'Of course.' Irene looked surprised

that Kate should question her decision. 'What else are friends for? I'll go home and pack a bag. I'm sure Fergal will drop me back here.'

'I could come back with you. It'll save bothering Fergal.'

'No, I'm sure there are things you'll need to do. Fergal won't mind. He sounded very concerned about you.'

'Did he?' She knew she sounded surprised, but she couldn't help herself. But was Irene telling her the truth? She'd thought Fergal was just furious with her.

★ ★ ★

It didn't take Irene long to go home and pack her few things. And she was right, it did give Kate the opportunity to quickly clean the spare room and make up the bed with clean linen. She'd just finished when the sound of a car pulling up outside alerted her to Fergal and Irene's arrival. She flew down the stairs and opened the door.

Only Irene stood there, suitcase at her feet. Fergal was already climbing back into the car. He turned and gave a brief wave, a cool smile, and was instantly gone again.

'Have you upset him?' Irene curiously asked, watching the car disappear round the bend in the lane.

'I don't think so,' was all Kate could say. How could she tell Irene the truth of what had happened? Irene would probably call her all sorts of a fool.

'Hmm.' Irene clearly didn't believe her.

'Come in, I'll put the kettle on.'

'Lovely. Just what I need.'

As Kate laid a tray with three cups and saucers, Irene asked, 'Expecting someone?'

'Yes. I'm sure Dan will be here in a couple of minutes. He usually spots anyone visiting me and then calls in as well.' She hoped Irene didn't detect the irony in her tone.

'Really!' She eyed Kate curiously. 'Still, it must be a comfort to know that he's watching over you?'

Kate didn't reply. For the truth was, Dan's constant surveillance, combined with his self-appointed guardianship, was beginning to feel oppressive. It was as if she had no private life any more.

Just as she had warned, it took precisely five minutes for the doorbell to ring once more. Irene cocked an eyebrow at her over her tea cup. Amusement glinted in her eye. 'Dan, I presume?'

'I expect so.'

She ushered him in. 'I was expecting you.'

Dan too failed to detect the irony in her tone.

'I thought I saw you go by in Cameron's car,' were Dan's first words to Irene. No polite preliminaries such as 'Hello, how are you?' or 'Nice to see you again'. No, straight to the point. It was almost as if he were becoming obsessed with Fergal.

His next words seemed to bear this out. As his glance strayed round the room, he asked, 'Has he gone then? Only I didn't see him pass by again.'

'No, he carried on along the lane. Not enough room to turn.'

'Right. So . . . ' he did have the grace to turn back to Irene then, 'come for the afternoon? I would imagine Kate's glad of the company.'

'Actually, Irene's staying for a few days.'

'Oh? How come?' He stared at Kate, no expression on his face at all; not even one of curiosity. 'It's a bit close to home for a holiday venue.' He smiled.

'I thought Kate needed the company of a friend, Dan. Not that you aren't just along the lane,' Irene hurriedly added, seeing the frown of displeasure that instantly tugged at Dan's brow. 'Still, next door isn't the same as having someone in the house, is it?'

'No, I suppose not,' was Dan's reluctant concession to that. He did look slightly mollified by Irene's words, however. 'Although, I would have been only too happy to come — '

'Yes,' Kate cut him off. 'I know you would have, Dan, but it's a woman's company that I need at the present time.'

'I see.' He didn't sound too pleased about that. In fact, he sounded positively resentful.

'Cup of tea?'

★ ★ ★

Eventually Dan left, a little happier in mood. 'I must say,' he told Kate upon leaving, 'I'll feel better knowing there's someone here. But I want you to promise that you'll phone me if anything untoward happens, anything at all. After all,' he practically smirked, 'I can't imagine Irene being much good in any sort of emergency. She's just a frail old lady.'

Kate glanced anxiously towards the sitting room where Irene had remained. If she'd heard that remark, she'd have apoplexy. Irene prided herself on her energy and stamina. Quite rightfully, in Kate's opinion. She was wonderful for a seventy-eight-year-old. Look at how she'd taken part in the Box Wood protest. No sign of trepidation or fear. In stark contrast to Kate's diffidence.

'OK, Dan,' she hurriedly agreed, for fear of what else he'd say. 'I promise.'

Irene stayed for a full week. In spite of Dan's pronouncement that she was too close to home for it to be a holiday, that exactly what it turned into — for both of them. They ventured out and about in Kate's car, Irene directing her to places she hadn't known existed.

Then, they took Jess on walks; walks that were slower and shorter than Kate's usually were — in deference to Irene's arthritis. Jess loved it, however, having both the people that she adored with her and gradually, as the week went by, Kate's fears began to subside. Especially as nothing at all happened to disturb the peace and tranquillity of life in Bower Cottage.

There were no phone calls, other than of the welcome kind, no anonymous letters, and no unwelcome visitors. Even

Dan kept his distance. Maybe, just maybe, Kate began to think, this would be an end to it all.

Of course, eventually, Irene had to go home. She had her own life to lead, her own friends to see. Kate drove her back, genuinely sorry to see the old lady go. It had been almost like having a mother with her again. A more loving, gentler mother; less critical than her own had sometimes been. Kate helped her into the house and kissed her. 'Thank you so much, Irene. I feel so much better now. I've enjoyed your company more than I can say.'

She drove home in a reflective mood. The cottage was going to seem a lonelier place now — for a day or two, at least. It was as she went inside that the phone started to ring. She smiled to herself. Irene, ringing to check that she was all right on her own again.

'Hello?' she said. There was no answer. She replaced the receiver slowly, a sense of dread beginning to creep over her. It rang again, and for the second time there was no answer. When it rang a third time, she picked it up and cried, 'Leave me alone — whoever you are, leave me alone,' and she slammed the receiver down.

It rang again and again. Each time she ignored it. It wasn't until it finally stopped that she buried her face in her hands and succumbed to helpless tears.

She was right back where she'd started. Despair engulfed her. She couldn't bear it. It was beginning all over again.

★   ★   ★

The following day, she returned from her morning walk to discover her front door standing open and an envelope lying on the floor inside. She picked it up and tore it open, her heart thumping.

YOU NEED BETTER LOCKS. IF I CAN GET IN THIS EASILY, WHO KNOWS WHAT ELSE I CAN DO? BE WARNED.

Within an hour, she'd had all of her door locks changed, plus locks fitted to every window. She didn't tell anyone this time. What was the point? It was glaringly evident that no-one could stop any of this happening. All she could do was wait. Wait and see what whoever it was behind it all wanted. Because want something they surely did, and sooner or later they'd have to tell her what it was, otherwise what was the point of it all?

At least the phone calls had stopped after her outburst the last time. Of course, eventually the phone did ring again and it was with a trembling hand that she lifted the receiver. 'Ye-es?'

Silence greeted her, apart from the sound of someone breathing.

'Hello?' she said again. There was still no answer. She replaced the phone, where upon it rang again almost at once.

She snatched it up. 'Yes; hello? Hello?' When no-one answered for the third time, she cried again, 'What do you want? Tell me!' Silence. 'Oh, just leave me alone then!' and she slammed down the receiver.

★ ★ ★

When the phone did eventually ring again, Kate stared at it for several long seconds, before, with fingers that shook so badly she could barely grasp it, she lifted the receiver. 'Ye-es?'

'Kate?' It was Fergal. 'Are you all right? You sound — shaky; nervous. Oh no. You haven't had another brick through the window, have you?' He sounded perfectly normal, no trace of the cool distance he'd shown upon dropping Irene off. Really, the man was like a chameleon.

Only, instead of changing colour at a second's notice, he changed moods. Nonetheless, she breathed a sigh of relief at the sound of his voice. The truth was, she needed all the friends she could get at the moment.

'No. I've had a few more silent phone

calls, though.' She sounded a whole lot calmer than she felt. In reality, her nerves were strung to breaking point. 'I stopped picking up for a while.'

'Very sensible. I don't know what to suggest.'

His concern transmitted itself down the phone line, warming and comforting her. He sounded so genuinely worried by it all. Her tormentor couldn't be him, surely? She so wanted to believe that.

'Should you call the police? Maybe they can trace whoever it was?'

His words underlined her faith that the culprit wasn't him. Because if it was, surely, he wouldn't suggest contacting the police to ask if they could trace the anonymous caller? Unless it was an enormous bluff, of course? Sounding honest and concerned purely and simply to fool her? 'They haven't been very successful tracing anything else so I can't see much point in reporting it.'

'Hmm, well, I'm not so sure about

that. By the way, did everything go okay with Irene — you know, having her to stay? It must have been reassuring to have someone there. Not to be alone after all that had happened.'

'Yes, it was. We had a great time.'

'Good. Anyway,' he paused, as if unsure whether to go on, which was a tad unusual for Fergal. Normally, he was so self-assured, so confident that whatever he was about to do was the right thing. Kate waited with baited breath for whatever it was he was about to say.

'On a lighter note, I've got a couple of tickets for the local golf club's summer ball. They've been harder to get hold of than stardust this year — everyone's wanted to go. I wondered if you'd like to come with me? I meant to say something the other day when I rang but then, with what had happened, I forgot all about it. Mind you, I hadn't even got the tickets at that point, so it could have been a mite premature.'

To say she was surprised would be an

understatement of quite massive pro-
portions. But all of a sudden, she
realised there was nothing she'd like
more. 'Oh Fergal, I'd love to. When is
it?'

'Rather short notice, I'm afraid. The
day after tomorrow. As I said, I've only
just managed to get tickets.'

'Oh, goodness!'

'It's not terribly formal. I mean, it
doesn't have to be a ball gown — just
smart cocktail wear.

'Oh well, in that case . . . '

'I'll pick you up at seven o'clock.
There's always a rather good buffet by
the way, so don't bother eating before
we go.'

★   ★   ★

A frantic search through her wardrobe
revealed that she had nothing remotely
suitable to wear. Kate groaned. She'd
got rid of a lot of her things prior to her
move, promising herself a spending
spree as soon as she had the time and

had never got round to it. Mainly because she'd had no real need of new clothes.

Well, she'd make the time now. She'd go to Worcester and treat herself to something really glamorous. It was time she had a treat and it would help take her mind off her troubles.

It took Kate no time at all to find the perfect dress. It was a dream — without being over-the-top. It was also horrendously expensive, more than she'd ever paid for a single garment before.

'It was made for you,' the sales assistant told her. 'It's crying out for a figure like yours.'

Kate needed no second bidding. Expensive or no, it was her dress. She had to have it. 'I'll take it,' she said.

'I'm sure you won't regret it,' the girl told her.

And she didn't. She viewed herself in the mirror on the evening of the ball and decided it had been worth every penny.

Made of shaded honey and cream

chiffon, the dress heightened the green of her eyes, turning them to jade, as well as intensifying the natural tones of her skin, making it look creamy and smoother than usual.

She frowned at her reflection, trying to view herself through Fergal's eyes. Would he perceive it as a signal that she would belatedly welcome his kisses; was inviting them, in fact?

Her spirit lifted at the prospect of an entire evening spent in his company. Oh Lord. Was she falling for him, despite her reservations? Oh well. Neither that nor anything else was going to stand in the way of her enjoying herself this evening. It was just what she needed. An evening spent in the company of a handsome man.

Although, heaven knows what Dan would think — or say, come to that — when he knew. A worrying question occurred to her then. Would he be at the ball? He was a member of the golf club, after all. She swallowed nervously. If he was — would he make a scene? It seemed likely, given his extreme antipathy towards Fergal — especially when it concerned anything to do with her.

For the first time then she wondered whether it was simply jealousy that caused the hostility between the two men? Jealousy over her? It would seem reasonable to suppose that in the case of Dan. He'd exhibited that emotion many times now.

But Fergal? She couldn't imagine him experiencing an emotion as primitive as jealousy. And certainly not over her. He always seemed so sure of himself. Yet — he had kissed her. So he must feel something.

She'd just picked up the soft shrug that she'd bought specially to wrap round her shoulders and slipped it on, when the doorbell chimed. Fergal. Her heart skipped a beat as she went to greet him.

Kate And Fergal Share
A Tender Moment

To Kate's relief Dan wasn't anywhere to be seen when she and Fergal arrived at the luxurious hotel in which the ball was being held. Fairy lights had lined the long driveway up to it and Chinese lanterns were threaded through the branches of the trees in front of the colonnaded entrance.

It made for a very romantic setting and Dan's presence would have cast a distinct dampener upon the evening for Kate. His antipathy towards Fergal was becoming more and more marked, increasing her certainty that simple jealousy was the root cause.

Which would have more or less ensured that the sight of Kate, clasped tightly in Fergal's arms as they danced, would have been more than sufficient to provoke some sort of scene. As it was, Kate wished the evening would go on forever. For it was living up to every one of her expectations.

Her dress had proved a huge success, the gleam that appeared in Fergal's dark eyes leaving her in no doubt that he approved. She hadn't been able to resist slanting a glance towards him as she'd locked the front door behind her.

He'd looked even more handsome than usual in his dark trousers and dinner jacket. Was this wise? she asked herself then, for the umpteenth time. To spend a whole evening, alone with the man she was growing increasingly attracted to? Without having the foggiest idea of how he really felt about her — despite the passion with which he'd kissed her. And without him having the foggiest idea about her circumstances.

Yet here she was, head only an inch or so away from his broad shoulder, feeling as if she'd reached heaven in just moments. All of which ensured that by the time he led her back to their table, her hand still in his, the thing she'd feared was happening. She was perilously close to falling in love.

They'd talked easily over a supper that turned out to be a truly magnificent buffet, about anything and everything, yet not really touching upon the personal.

Kate decided to put that right. She wanted to know everything about him. What made him tick? What his family were like? What his ambitions were for the future?

He pulled out a chair for her and she sat down. He topped her wine glass up.

And then, it was as if Fergal had made the same decision she had, because his first question upon sitting down was, 'So — Kate, I've never asked you, and I have to admit to some curiosity. What made you come here from Birmingham? I mean, it's such a contrast. Bright lights to darkness. Hustle bustle to silence.'

'That's exactly why I did it. I was tired of the frantic pace of life. Everyone rushing here, there and everywhere — and for what? Very little when you examine things closely. I needed a change.'

She felt a stab of guilt. Here she was preparing to quiz him about his life when, in answer to the first question he asked her, she'd lied. She could appease her conscience by telling him part of the truth, however, even if it was an abridged version. 'And I came into some money.'

'Lucky girl!' He grinned at her, it was a rakish grin, devastatingly attractive. Kate felt her heart leap.

'Not really. My parents died within eighteen months of each other.'

She saw the gold flecks appear in his eyes as he reached over the table and folded his fingers around hers. 'Not so lucky then. I'm sorry.'

'They left me some money and, of course, their house. I sold it and, well, to cut a long story short — here I am.'

The truth teetered perilously on the edge of her tongue. She so wanted to tell him all of it. But how could she after all this time? And here? Whatever would he think of her? 'Um, I've often won-dered — your businesses, the garages and showrooms, the hotels, etcetera. Did you build it all up from scratch?'

He showed no sign of minding her abrupt change of subject from her own affairs to his. 'I bought several of the garages after they'd gone bust. The others, I bought as going concerns, the last one just twelve months ago. Nearly broke me,' his glance was rueful. 'It's been hard going at times but worth it. That's not to say that there aren't times when I couldn't do with some more cash, but then, we all suffer from that these days.' He tilted his head to one side. 'Or maybe not.' He laughed then; it was a heart-warming sound. 'I am, after all, sitting across from a woman who is wealthy in her own right. You don't meet too many of those.'

'Oh dear, I may have given you the wrong impression. Comfortable would be a more apt description than wealthy. I wouldn't want to mislead you.'

But his words, as light-hearted as

he'd made them sound, only deepened Kate's guilt about her deception. Tell him, her instincts bade her. Tell him — now. But right at the last second her nerve failed and once again she chickened out.

★   ★   ★

It was as they were walking back to his car at the end of the evening, a silver-blue Jaguar, that he reached for her hand and took hold of it.

'Thank you for coming, Kate. I've really enjoyed your company.'

'I've enjoyed myself too, Fergal. Thank you for inviting me.'

Their steps had slowed while this exchange had been going on and, all of a sudden, they found themselves facing each other, hands clasped between them. Fergal leant towards her and gently kissed her cheek.

Then, he gave a small groan and murmured, 'I'm sorry — I can't help myself — you're so sweet, Kate, so lovely.'

He curved an arm around her waist, pulling her close as his head lowered to hers, and, in the next instant, he was kissing her.

But then — she couldn't do this — not till he knew the truth about her, and how could she tell him that now — after all this time? He'd despise her for her deception, her guile — quite rightly. She wrenched herself free.

'Kate! What's the matter? Tell me.' He looked angry now rather than offended. 'Do you have something against me?'

Miserably, she shook her head. 'No. You don't understand.'

'Then tell me. Make me understand.'

'I-I can't. Sorry — I just can't. It's too late.'

He turned away from her. A tiny sob shook her slender frame. What a mess she'd got herself into.

They drove back to the cottage in silence.

'Here we are — home.' Fergal's voice was glacial. It contradicted his look of fury. She couldn't blame him. Both times she'd led him to believe that she cared about him and was interested in some sort of relationship. What must he think of her?

Kate sat back in the seat. She could see the front of her cottage, its small windows gleaming silver in the moonlight. It looked like something out of a fairytale, which should mean that the heroine found her true love, her prince, and lived happily ever after.

She sighed. Only in her case, that could never happen. She had too big a secret; she'd told too many lies. The prince would never be able to forgive that.

Fergal climbed from the car and walked round to open her door. 'I'll see you in.'

'Thank you.'

They walked in silence, one behind the other, to her front door. And it wasn't until she was inside that Kate gave way to her despair. The tears slid, one after another, down her cheeks.

Jess came to her and nuzzled her legs. She crouched down and, putting both arms around the animal, rubbed her wet face into warm fur. 'I'm being silly, Jess, take no notice of me.' All she seemed to do these days was weep — and she'd never been the weepy sort. It just went to show the state of mind she was in.

Eventually, her tears did dry and she prepared herself for bed, longing for the reprieve from her unhappiness that slumber would provide. She'd just settled with a book, hoping to take her mind off Fergal and his shuttered expression as he'd said goodnight, when the phone at her side rang.

She couldn't help it. The hope that it was the man she'd just left calling her wouldn't be suppressed. Maybe he was going to apologise for the abrupt way in which he'd left her? With a hand that shook, she lifted the receiver to her ear. 'Yes?'

There was no answer, other than the sounds of breathing.

A Face From The Past

Kate signed the cheque and then stared uncertainly down at it. Was this the right thing to do? It was a lot of money — would Sally see it as a gift, meant sincerely, or as an insult? A bribe? Or was that what she'd been working towards all along?

She couldn't rid herself of the suspicion that it might be Sally behind the stalking, the intimidation, the sheer persecution. But she also found herself wondering if, despite the way their friendship had ended, rather acrimoniously, whether Sally was really the sort of person who would be capable of something like this? Capable of terrorising her friend?

They'd been friends for so long, ever since their schooldays, in fact. And Sally had been a rock in the aftermath of her mother's death. Kate didn't know what she'd have done without her. All of this — well, it seemed so out of character for Sally.

Yet, the truth was — she'd changed the moment she'd discovered that Kate had indeed read the lottery numbers correctly and was about to be the possessor of a veritable fortune. Kate had always heard that money didn't automatically bring happiness with it. She now knew that to be true.

She sighed and slowly slid the cheque into an envelope with the already prepared note, saying who it was from. *I think I owe you this.* Please accept it. She sealed the envelope, and, still frowning with indecision, attached a first class stamp to it.

'Come on, Jess,' she then called.

The dog bounded forward, eager as ever for their morning walk. Kate attached the lead to her collar and together they left the house. Half an hour later, the deed was done. She'd slipped the envelope into the post box. Now, it was impossible for her to change her mind.

If she was right in her suspicion, the phone calls, the stalking, the terrorising would now cease. If it didn't — well, she'd have to seriously reconsider her position — here in the village that she'd grown to love. Have to consider moving again, to somewhere where, once again, no-one would know her. Yet, who was to say that the same thing wouldn't happen again?

★   ★   ★

A couple of days went by without an incident of any sort. She didn't know whether she was pleased about that or not. It meant that the culprit most likely had been Sally and she simply didn't know how she felt about that.

If her best friend could do such a thing to her, what would other people be capable of?

It was on the third day after she'd posted the letter that there came a knock on her door. Jess was instantly on her feet — the dog was now almost as jumpy as Kate — as a soft growl rumbled deep in her throat.

'Ssh, Jess, it's OK.' She hoped she was right in that assurance. In case she wasn't, she did what she always did now before opening the door, she went to the window that overlooked the front garden and peered out. 'Oh, my goodness!' she cried.

She ran to the door and yanked it open — rather unwisely, she later reflected. What if her suspicions about Sally were true. Who knew what dangers she would have been opening her door to? 'Sally! What on earth are you doing here?'

Her friend gave a tentative smile and waved a piece of paper at her. It was the cheque that Kate had sent her.

'I thought I'd return this — in person. Oh, Kate,' her face crumpled, 'I'm so sorry for what I did. For the way I behaved. You owe me noth — ' Her voice broke as the tears spilled down her face.

She gave a small hiccup and visibly fought for control. 'You owe me nothing, absolutely nothing. You won the money, fair and square.' The tears returned. She dashed them away. 'Can you ever forgive me?'

'Oh, Sally.' Kate held out her arms, her own face now awash with tears. 'Of course I can. Come here.'

Sally literally dived into the open arms and buried her face in Kate's shoulder, openly sobbing now. 'I've missed you so much.'

'Come on, come inside. I've missed you too — terribly. If you only knew how much. Oh Sally, I've needed you so badly. My rock — ' The tears spilled over again, tears of utmost relief as well as happiness. This proved her persecutor wasn't Sally. If it had been, she'd have kept the money — wouldn't she? 'Oh no, all I do is cry lately. Sorry — She dashed the tears away. 'Sorry.'

Sally drew back and frowned at her friend's forlorn face. 'What's happened? What do you mean? All you do is cry?

Why? You've never been the weepy sort.'

'Huh! You should see me now. I can't seem to stop. Come in and I'll put the kettle and tell you everything. Oh dear, the relief of being able to talk about it all.'

Sally's face was a picture of curiosity and confusion, all mixed up with genuine anxiety. More proof, if she needed it, that it hadn't been Sally behind it all.

Over their cups of tea it all came spilling out. How she'd decided not to reveal her lottery win — to anyone. All the horrible things that had been happening to her. Her thankfulness at having her dearest friend with her and being able to talk it all over, share her nightmare, drove away her fears — at least, temporarily.

'But someone knows who I am, Sally,' she concluded. 'Which isn't terrible on its own, I could live with that. No, the question that strikes fear into me is — what do they want? Why don't they come clean and say they know? That's what makes it all so — sinister, so threatening.'

'Quite,' Sally thoughtfully agreed. 'And if it was money they wanted, surely they've have demanded it by now?'

'My thoughts exactly. That's what makes it all so frightening. What do they want? To scare me out of my mind? They've succeeded. So, why not come out into the open and tell me what I have to do?'

'Do you have any suspects at all? Think carefully.'

'Not really.' Kate decided not to tell her that she had been suspect-in-chief for quite a while now. She wasn't sure how Sally would react to that. She might laugh uproariously, or she might not. It could just kill off the fragile budding of their renewed friendship.

She did describe her friends, however, all of them.

'It can't be one of them, can it? Oh Sally, I've been such a fool. I should have been upfront and honest from the beginning, trusted them to like me for myself. Trusted myself in that I'm likeable enough — '

She bowed her head into her hands. 'If I'd done that, no-one would have the means to threaten me with anything. Because everyone would already know the truth. But if I admit the truth now — what's it going to look like?'

'They'll all have you down as a deceitful minx, you mean?'

'Yes. And I'll lose my friends.'

'Oh, Kate. This is partly my fault. If I hadn't behaved so badly, you wouldn't now be paranoid about telling people.' Sally hugged her. 'But hey! I'm sure you won't lose your friends. They probably — no, change that to most certainly genuinely like you for yourself. You're such a special person. What's not to like? Huh? They won't care about your little deception — I'm sure they'll understand.'

'Well, I'm not. And I've already upset one of them: Fergal.'

'Have you? How? You haven't accused him?' Sally looked shocked.

'Erm, no — well, not really. Not accused, no — '

'Oh, dear, what then? What have you done?'

But Kate couldn't bring herself to tell even her best friend about the kisses. 'Oh, you know.'

'No, I don't. Tell me.'

'It's nothing — really. And I'm sure he'll get over it. Not that I care whether he does or not . . . ' and she shrugged.

It was, of course, a complete lie, but Sally wasn't to know that.

Sally didn't press her. Instead, she gave a small smile and said, 'OK, you don't want to talk about it. That's fine. Um, changing the subject, completely,' Sally said, 'I've got a bag in the car.'

'Bag?' Kate was puzzled.

'Yeah. A bag of clothes. I could stay a while. I've got some holiday time to take.'

'Oh, Sally, could you?' Kate breathed. It was exactly what she needed. A few days for intimate, catch-up chats with her very best friend.

'Sure can. I'll go and fetch it from the car.'

'Sally,' Kate called after her, 'you will keep the secret. I want to be the one to tell everyone, and I will — soon; very soon.'

Sally looked back at her, her cheeks flushed pink, 'Don't worry, I've no intention of making that mistake again. But, seriously, the sooner you tell people, the sooner this — character will have no reason to blackmail you — if that's what he's doing,' and she frowned as she strode to the car.

★ ★ ★

For Kate, it was wonderful simply having Sally there. They had so much to tell each other. Sally had been promoted to position of manageress of the cafe, the position that Kate had been proud possessor of. It had meant that Sally could move up the housing ladder and rent herself a better flat.

'Mind you, it's a hovel compared to this,' she said, indicating the inglenook fireplace, the multitude of darkened beams, the comfortable furniture that sat in the sitting room. 'This is gorgeous.'

Kate looked carefully for any signs of envy, of resentment, but there were none. She breathed a tiny sigh of contentment. Sally had never been a covetous person — at least, not until Kate had had her enormous win. Thank goodness all evidence of that had vanished. Sally looked simply happy for her now.

'It is, isn't it?' Kate agreed. 'It's what I've always wanted.'

'Really! I didn't know that. I'd never had you down as a traditionalist.'

Their chatting was interrupted by a rap on the front door.

'Just a sec',' Kate said, 'I'll see who it is.' But she didn't have to open the door to know who it was.

Sure enough, it was Dan. She was

surprised it had taken him two days to call. For sure, he would have seen her and Sally passing his house. As she'd decided more than once, he must keep a more or less permanent watch of passing traffic — and people.

'Why, Dan. Fancy you being here.' Her tongue was thrust deep into the side of her cheek as she said this.

Fortunately, her sarcasm went over his head. He was much more interested in the sight of Sally's head poking out of the sitting room doorway as she attempted to see beyond Kate to whomever it was standing there.

'Oh, you've got company,' Dan exclaimed. For all the word as if that fact had come as a complete surprise to him.

However, he almost at once betrayed himself by adding, 'I thought you must have when I spotted you out walking with someone.'

Kate suppressed a smile and said, 'Would you like to come in and meet my company?'

Dan all but bounded through the doorway, such was his eagerness to meet Sally.

'This is Sally, my oldest and dearest friend,' Kate said. 'Sally, meet Dan, my nearest neighbour.'

'Your only neighbour,' Dan chipped in. 'And I trust you consider me a dear friend also.'

'Of course,' Kate conceded. 'Sally's going to be staying a while — she just turned up on the doorstep. It was a wonderful surprise.'

'Oh?' Dan regarded first Kate and then Sally with a strange expression. If Kate had been pressed to describe it, she would have said he wasn't best pleased at this news.

'Dan has been very kind, and very helpful,' Kate told Sally.

'How nice,' Sally said, coming closer and holding out a hand to Dan.

Dan took it. 'It's nice to meet you too, um — Sally.

'Please come in and sit down, Dan,' Kate invited. 'We're having a cup of tea.

Would you like one?'

'Well,' Dan looked thoughtful for a second, 'I've just had one.' A smile, however, almost immediately banished the expression. 'How long are you staying?' he bluntly asked Sally, and in not too friendly a manner.

Sally practically choked on her tea. 'Um — another few days,' she managed to say, once she'd got her breath back, 'or shall we say till Kate's had enough and throws me out.' She grinned broadly at her friend.

'That will never happen,' Kate smiled back. 'You can stay as long as you want — forever, if you like,' she finished.

'I see.' Dan eyed Sally. 'Obviously, you knew where Kate lived.'

'Well, yes,' Sally answered,' otherwise how would I have known where to come?' She directed a small and very puzzled frown at Kate.

'Has Kate told you what's been happening to her?'

'Yes, she has. And if you ask me, it's a good thing I've arrived.'

'Oh, why's that?' Dan asked, rather sharply.

It was now Kate's turn to frown at him. What on earth was wrong with him? Oh no. The answer had just occurred to her. Dan suspected — just as she had for a while she had to admit — that the culprit was Sally.

'Dan . . . ' she began, unsurely.

Sally interrupted. 'Because, maybe, between us we can catch whoever it is — send him packing with a flea in his miserable little ear.'

'Oh,' Dan's eyebrow flew upwards. 'You assume it's a he then?'

'It doesn't sound like something that a woman would do. Standing around in corners, putting the fear of God into someone.' She snorted contemptuously. 'It's the sort of thing some inadequate, sad man would do. It probably makes him feel powerful.'

'So, you don't think women are capable of wickedness then? Just as capable of crime as a man?'

'I'm sure some are, but not many.

Anyway, Kate says it was definitely a man she saw, so — ' Sally shrugged, ' — case proven, in my opinion.'

Dan didn't say anything for a while. He simply stood, a hand on each hip, regarding Sally thoughtfully. 'So, are you thinking of becoming her bodyguard?'

'If necessary,' Sally defiantly said, meeting his gaze head-on.

Dan's gaze swept over her, somewhat contemptuously it had to be said. 'Bit small for that job, aren't you? And in any case, Kate doesn't want a bodyguard. Lord knows, I've offered myself in that capacity more than once and she always refuses. She doesn't want to be intimidated, she says. Refuses to be intimidated, in fact.'

'Dan!' Kate cried.

'I'm sure she'll want me — her oldest friend — to watch over her.' Sally's ire had been aroused, well and truly. 'Someone she can really trust.'

'Sally!' Kate was in despair. This was the last thing she wanted, her two friends squabbling over her.

'Are you suggesting I can't be trusted?' Dan furiously demanded.

'No, Dan, of course she isn't.' Kate directed a glare of reproach at Sally. What on earth was happening here?

They both ignored her. 'I've told her — time and time again — to come to me. But will she?' Dan snorted. 'I mean — what's the use of having a neighbour, a fairly strong, fit man, I might add,' here he actually smirked at Sally, 'if she refuses to make use of him.'

'Please — ' Kate pleaded. 'Both of you calm down.'

'Oh, don't worry, Kate,' Dan sneered, 'with Little Miss Angel here, you won't have any need of me, so I'll just take myself off, shall I?'

'Dan, please. Let's just . . . ' But she was too late, Dan had left, storming off along the driveway.

'Whoops,' Sally said. 'What a pompous twit! Is he always like that?'

Kate smiled ruefully as she closed the

door. 'Not usually, no. But he can get a bit possessive.'

'Possessive!' Sally cried. 'I'd call that a bit more than possessive. The man's actually jealous of me being here with you. My Lord, Kate, he's well and truly obsessed with you.'

'He's been very good — watching out for me.'

'Are you sure he's not been watching you all the time?'

Kate frowned again. 'What do you mean?'

'Well, he's so possessive; could it have been him stalking you? It would be a very effective way of keeping a check on you and everything you're doing?'

'Dan! No; never. No way. It's not in Dan's nature. All right, I admit he can be a bit — well, intense, but no, he isn't capable of such behaviour. Definitely not.'

'Hmm,' Sally sipped at her tea, her gaze reflective now as it lingered on her friend.

Another Visitor Arrives

'My word,' Kate murmured, when she saw who it was walking along the pathway to the front door, 'the tom-tom drums have been busy.'

'Well, if you choose to live in a small village!'

'Fergal,' Kate said as she opened the door, a little apprehensively it had to be said. They hadn't exactly parted on good terms the last time they'd seen each other. In fact, the terms had been about as bad as they could get. No wonder he hadn't been in touch.

Sally, as was her wont, also sped to the door, her eyes lighting up at the sight of such a good looking man. 'Wow!' she whispered from right behind Kate. 'Now this one is definitely worth meeting. You didn't tell me he was this gorgeous. If he wants to be your bodyguard, I would advise you to accept. And if you don't want him, I do.'

Kate manfully maintained a straight face, while surreptitiously elbowing her friend in the ribs.

Fergal, of course, couldn't miss Sally's face peering round Kate. 'Sorry,' he said, 'I didn't realise you had a visitor. Shall I come back?'

'No, no,' Sally eagerly put in, darting round to the front of Kate and pulling Fergal through the doorway. 'I'm Sally, Kate's closest friend. So nice to meet you,' she gushed.

Kate closed her eyes in resignation. Not surprisingly. Because to say Fergal looked taken aback would be an understatement. He looked positively stunned. However, when she opened her eyes again, it was to see him regarding her with quiet amusement. Well, at least he wasn't about to freeze her with the sort of expression he seemed to specialise in. The one that reminded her so powerfully of the Arctic wastes. So, that was an improvement.

'Come in, Fergal,' Kate said — totally superfluously, as Sally was already leading him into the sitting room. 'I'm surprised Irene didn't tell you Sally was here. We called in to see her.'

'I haven't seen Irene,' he said.

'Cup of tea?' Sally butted in.

'Well — ' Fergal looked doubtful.

'How come you're not at work?' Kate asked.

'A meeting I'd had planned was cancelled so I thought I'd finish early — and come and see you. Have a chat — '

'About what?' The question was entirely unnecessary. She knew exactly what it would be about. About their last time together. Maybe he was going to apologise? Or, on the other hand, maybe not? She couldn't, for the life of her, imagine that many women would have rebuffed his advances — so he wouldn't be accustomed to saying sorry.

He took the cup of tea that Sally was proffering. Again, Kate closed her eyes. He probably had them down as a

257

couple of giggling girls.

'So — where are you from, Sally?' Fergal asked.

'Oh, good ole Brum, same as Kate. We know each other from way back. I thought it was time for a catch-up — I've been here for a few days now. I'm surprised we haven't met before this.' She looked accusingly at Kate. As if that omission were entirely Kate's fault. Kate glared back at her.

'Well, it's very nice, very nice, indeed, to meet you now. I'm just surprised that Kate's never mentioned you.' Fergal said, slightly bemusedly.

'She can be extremely forgetful,' Sally said, with a wicked glint to her eye.

'Well, there's forgetfulness and there's complete amnesia.' There was a decided glint to Fergal's eye now. 'I certainly wouldn't have thought she'd forget some-one as — memorable as you.'

Sally quite literally preened herself then. The glitter intensified within Fergal's eye. It was more than obvious that he liked what he saw with regards to Sally. Kate felt a lowering of spirit. She couldn't really blame him. Sally was everything she wasn't. Lively, pretty, witty. And, more importantly, without a history of deceit behind her.

There'd be absolutely nothing to stop her from beginning a relationship with him. And Fergal looked more than ready to comply with that. His lips twitched in a provocative grin as he watched Sally.

'I wonder,' he murmured, 'whether you'd allow me to take you both out for dinner tonight?'

'We certainly would,' Sally retorted.

'Well, I don't know about.' Kate began.

'Ignore her.' Sally blithely waved away Kate's low murmur of objection. 'Of course we'll come — won't we, Kate?' And she directed a particularly meaningful glance Kate's way. A glance that said, 'Don't be a party pooper'.

So what else could Kate do but reluctantly agree? 'Thank you, Fergal, we'd like that.'

'What time will you pick us up?'

Kate silently groaned. Sally had never been backward in coming forward.

'Eight o'clock?' Fergal said.

At last, his gaze left Sally and turned to Kate. Kate felt her insides begin to shrivel. His eyes were perfectly cool. Gone was the glitter of attraction that they'd held when he'd looked at Sally. Mr Arctic was well and truly back. Perhaps not surprisingly. He'd clearly sensed Kate's unwillingness to accept his invitation.

'Fine,' she answered shortly. Two could play at that game. Although what good it was going to do her, she didn't know. She'd lost her chance by the looks of it. Her two rejections of him had succeeded beyond her wildest dreams. He'd given up on her. She could have wept. And knowing she could blame no-one but herself didn't help; didn't help at all.

A Tense Evening

Running absolutely true to form, Sally, keen to make a good impression on the handsomest man she'd seen in an age, meticulously tried on every single garment she'd brought with her in her efforts to look just right for the evening ahead. Which took quite a time as it looked as if she'd brought practically every garment she owned with her.

'You've left out the kitchen sink,' Kate quipped at one point. Only to have to eventually hold out her wrist with its dainty wristwatch, tap it, and declare, 'We're not going to be ready if you go on like this.'

Finally, Sally plumped for an extremely short skirt. 'I've seen bigger pelmets than that' was Kate's initial reaction — teamed with a pastel silk top and a pair of extremely high heels. But even she had to admit that they did wonders for Sally's best feature, her incredibly shapely legs.

'You look gorgeous,' Kate told Sally. 'Come on then, are you ready? He'll be here any minute, and I wouldn't think Mr Fergal Cameron likes to be kept waiting.'

'Ooh, Miss Tetchy. What's he done to upset you?'

'Nothing.'

'Are you sure? I can tell by your expression he's done something.'

'Just leave it.' The doorbell rang, mercifully saving Kate from any further grilling by Sally. She knew only too well how persistent her friend could be. The proverbial mongrel and its bone came a poor second to Sally once she got her teeth into something.

★ ★ ★

Fergal took them to a nearby restaurant that Kate hadn't, as yet, been to. It was very discreet and very expensive, Kate suspected. Which probably explained why Dan hadn't chosen it for their date and had opted instead to embark upon a half hour journey to the other one. She swallowed.

She couldn't imagine Fergal accepting an offer to go halves with the bill. Yet, she felt she should. This emotion was boosted when the waiter brought the menus and she saw the prices. Almost ten pounds just for the starters. The main courses were double and even treble that.

'Wow!' Sally was gazing round with wide eyes. 'What a place! Who'd have thought you'd find somewhere like this out in the sticks.'

Kate raised her eyes to the ceiling at her friend's tactlessness, but Fergal simply laughed. He'd barely taken his eyes off Sally from the time he'd shown up at the cottage door.

Kate felt her spirits sink even lower. Between that and the prospect of a bill that would probably run into three figures, the evening was beginning to go downhill fast. She decided to offer to go halves. She really didn't want to be beholden to Fergal Cameron.

Especially not now, in the light of his obvious interest in her friend. In fact, she was starting to feel like the proverbial gooseberry. If she could have found some reason to leave them to it and return home she would have grabbed it — with both hands.

Instead, she cleared her throat and began, 'Um — I hope you'll let me contribute to this?' After all, she didn't know what Fergal's exact financial situation was, other than what he'd told her the night of the ball. And then, he'd seemed to suggest that he was a bit hard up. Whereas she — well, even though he didn't know it, she was a lottery winner.

Fergal turned his head away from Sally and looked at her. A frown pulled his brow downwards. 'Certainly not. I invited you out.'

'Well, yes — but there are two of us.'

'Kate,' he lowered his voice and leant towards her, 'I don't need a contribution, now leave it.'

Sally was far too busy studying the menu to have heard any of this, so it wasn't surprising that she should come in with, 'Oh boy. I hope you've got plenty of money on you, because this is going to cost a fortune!'

'Sally,' Kate moaned, acutely embarrassed by her friend's bluntness — just seconds after she herself had offered to pay something towards the final bill. Fergal would be thinking — what a pair of ignorant townies they were, and that he would have been better taking them to the nearest McDonald's — much more their scene.

'Sally, you are a girl after my own heart. You say what you're thinking — I like that, very much.' And he reached out to take hold of her one hand lying on the table top and squeeze it.

Sally, delighted with the way things were going, giggled, and squeezed back.

Kate stayed silent, trying very hard not to look at the two hands that had stayed intertwined for far longer than was necessary in her opinion. She looked everywhere else, around the room, at the other diners, she minutely inspected the decor, displayed a great interest in the pictures on the wall.

She was so engrossed in it all that she completely failed to see the manner in which Fergal looked at her. But Sally saw it, and very, very unobtrusively withdrew her hand from his. Fergal glanced at her in surprise. Sally raised a knowing eyebrow at him. He grinned back ruefully.

Kate remained oblivious to all of this. For her, the evening loomed miserably ahead; long and uncomfortable, with her wishing she were somewhere else; anywhere else but here, having to watch the pantomime being enacted in front of her.

For Sally quite simply couldn't help herself. Kate should have known she wouldn't be able to. She flirted madly, and Fergal — well, Fergal responded. She might as well not have been there, Kate gloomily reflected at one point.

As a consequence, she consumed her

meal in silence, only speaking when she was spoken to, and listening moodily to the banter of her companions. Their laughter was loud and unrestrained and invited many an amused — and one or two irritated — glances from the other diners.

Fergal and Sally remained oblivious to it all, however. They were engrossed in each other. Fergal did, at one point, seem to remember that Kate was there and remarked, 'You're very quiet.'

'I have a headache,' she snapped.

'Oh dear,' Fergal said. He instantly beckoned to the maître d'.

'Do you think I could have a couple of aspirins for my companion? She has a headache,' and he looked back at Kate with a small, but very knowing smile.

For two pins, Kate would have emptied her plate over his smug head. He knew only too well what was wrong with her; she knew that with utter conviction.

He was glorying in her misery; going out of his way, in fact, to provoke it.

Why? Something occurred to her then. Was he doing this deliberately? Flirting with Sally? It was beginning to look like it. But why? To punish her for her rejection of him? To make her jealous?

If that was the case, he was callously using Sally for his own ends, completely. Just as she'd suspected, Fergal Cameron wasn't accustomed to being refused anything. And he simply couldn't cope with it — to the extent of needing to exact some sort of cruel retribution, with no thought for the feelings of anyone whom he might be hurting in the process.

She looked at Sally now. Her friend's face was flushed with happiness. How could Fergal be so cruel? She wouldn't have thought that of him.

★ ★ ★

Eventually, the evening neared its end and Kate couldn't wait to get back to her cottage and the peace and quiet of her bedroom.

Fergal had deliberately humiliated her — by flirting outrageously all evening with Sally. Or was she doing him — and Sally, come to that — an injustice?

Maybe he really did want to start something with Sally? She was a lovely girl, with a gorgeous disposition. Any man would be pleased to count her as his girlfriend.

On the drive back, Fergal turned to Sally who was sitting in the front with him, Kate had insisted, preferring to sit wallowing in misery alone in the back, and asked, 'How long are you staying? We could perhaps do this again?'

Sally pulled a face. 'Sorry. I go back the day after tomorrow.'

'If you want to go out with Fergal one last time, Sally . . . ' Kate reluctantly said, 'go tomorrow. A farewell date.'

She disregarded the heaviness of her heart at the very idea of the two of them alone together. Maybe in each other's arms.

'Certainly not,' Sally riposted. 'Tomorrow night's for you and me, girl. A box of chocolates, a few hankies and a good blub. Nothing like it.'

'Oh, well, maybe we'll see you again soon,' was all Fergal said as he pulled up outside of Kate's gate.

'You sure will. Now I've found my way here,' and she opened the door and began to climb out.

Kate and Fergal followed suit and Fergal walked them to the door, where he put his arms around Sally and gave her a warm kiss. Was there any need to exhibit quite so much enjoyment of a simple kiss? Kate acrimoniously thought. Or to spend quite so much time over it?

He then turned to her and considered her thoughtfully for a long moment before leaning towards her and gently placing his lips against her cheek. 'Goodnight, Kate,' was all he said before turning back to Sally again, who, casting all inhibition to the four winds, flung her arms around him again and gave him a warm embrace, before saying, 'See you soon — hopefully.'

'I hope so too. I've very much enjoyed

your company,' and after a second's pause, 'the company of both of you, in fact.' He then gave her another kiss.

'Oh boy,' Sally breathed, looking up at him with shining eyes. 'If you do that too often, you'll never get rid of me.'

Fergal laughed, before turning to Kate, the smile quite gone from his face as he looked at her.

'Kate, I think you and I ought to have a talk — sometime soon.' His eyes gleamed, their expression unfathomable.

'I can't think what about,' Kate bit back.

An infinitesimal smile lifted the corners of his mouth. 'I'm sure you can — if you try hard enough.' And that was that.

He swung away, bestowed one last grin on Sally, and was gone.

'Oh boy,' Sally hugged herself ecstatically once they were inside. 'How do you stop yourself from falling head-over-heels in love with him?'

'Very easily.'

'Yeah? This is me, Kate, the friend

who knows you inside out, every little expression, every look. You can't fool me. You're in love with him — despite your display of indifference earlier.'

'No, I don't,' Kate indignantly contradicted.

'Yes, you do, otherwise why sulk all evening?'

'I wasn't sulking.' Again, she was all hot-cheeked indignation.

'Yes, you were. If you'd said you cared for him, I'd have kept well away.' Sally eyed her. 'Well, you don't have to be despondent. He feels exactly the same way.'

'What? You saw how he was with me. And the way he was so interested in you.'

'Yeah, to get you fired up. And it worked, didn't it? I would imagine he's extremely pleased with the way it all went. You couldn't have made your feelings more obvious if you'd taken out an advert in the local Gazette. The man's crazy about you. Still . . . ' she shrugged, 'I won't say I didn't enjoy the attention — even if it wasn't real. Look, my girl, stop messing about and grab him with both hands, before someone else does.'

All Kate could think, as she lay in bed half-an-hour later, was — could Sally possibly be right? Did Fergal return her feelings? Really? But, if he did, how on earth was he going to react when she told him the truth about herself? It would most likely wreck everything.

How could any man go on wanting a woman who'd done nothing but lie to him — almost from the first moment that she'd met him? She gave a groan of anguish. What was she going to do?

★　★　★

With Sally gone, the cottage felt very empty to Kate, and her fears resurrected themselves once more. Strangely, the persecution — intimidation, whatever you wanted to call it — had stopped completely while her friend had been there.

But then, it had also stopped while

Irene had been with her. Even so, Kate couldn't help reluctantly considering, for the umpteenth time, whether Sally had indeed had some part in it all. She'd finally been persuaded to accept the cheque that Kate had written for her so if it had been her, maybe it would all now stop?

But, if it hadn't been Sally behind it, maybe whoever it truly was had decided that any more torment wouldn't have the desired effect while Kate had someone with her, and so had halted the campaign — temporarily? In which case she'd have to wait and see if it started up again.

It didn't take long.

The very next night the phone rang. Without thinking, she picked it up. 'Hello?' There was just silence. She slammed it back down. When it rang a second time, she ignored it.

Kate Makes A Shocking Discovery

'I saw you going off with Cameron the other night.' Kate turned. It was Dan, standing looking over the hedge that bordered the front garden. She was cleaning windows, a task she hated, but the household chores had been sadly neglected in favour of restoring the garden and she had decided it was time to get down to some serious work.

It also took her mind off last night's silent call, as well as Sally's going and her words about Fergal being crazy about her. She still didn't know whether to believe Sally or not. Fergal hadn't been in touch to have that talk he'd referred to. Maybe he'd changed his mind and decided to leave things as they were? Perhaps, he'd decided he preferred Sally after all?

'He took Sally and me out for a meal.'

'No, before she arrived.'

He must be referring to the night of the golf club ball.

'Where were you going?'

'You must mean the summer ball at the golf club. I half expected to see you there.'

'It's not my scene — and I hadn't got a partner anyway. You know, you want to be careful of him.'

'Of who? Fergal? Why's that?' She continued with her window cleaning, feigning a lack of interest she was far from feeling. She wasn't sure she wanted to hear this.

'I've heard he's teetering on the verge of bankruptcy. Over extended himself, expanded too fast. And there you are.'

Angrily, Kate swung to face him again. 'Ye-es, here I am. So what?'

'Clearly a woman of means. Has he asked you for a loan yet? Maybe he's asked you to marry him? Nothing like bagging himself a rich wife.'

'I came into some money, Dan — that's it!' Kate cried. 'Most of which I've spent. That hardly makes me rich.' She couldn't believe that anyone could change as dramatically as Dan had. He'd started off by being so friendly. Now, he was bitter, possessive — resentful. It must be the jealousy that had done it? Jealousy of Fergal? She couldn't think of any other reason.

'Oh, come on. You're hardly on the breadline, Kate. I mean, you don't have a job, do you?'

'No, but I'm about to get one.' Kate stopped, horrified at what she'd just blurted out. Get a job? What job? Where?

'You're getting a job?' Dan blinked at her.

'We-ell, yes.' What a great idea. Why hadn't she considered it before? A job would get her out of the house, as well as give her something else to think of, other than the continuing threat of silent phone calls, broken windows, night-time intruders . . .

But it was obvious that Dan didn't believe her. 'What sort of job?' he scoffed. 'There aren't too many cafes in Great Mindon. Well, there is one, but it's so small the owner runs it single-handedly. I can't imagine she needs any extra staff, even someone as experienced as yourself. Of course, you could always offer to run it for her. Or maybe buy it. Despite what you say, I'm sure you could still afford it.'

It was just the spur Kate needed. 'I don't know yet what I'm going to do. Actually, I'm off to the nearest job centre this morning. At Oxbridge, I suppose.' Although she made it sound as if it was already decided, she'd only just thought of it. But why not? See what opportunities were on offer. She had nothing better to do, well — other than clean windows and almost any-thing would be an improvement on that. 'Maybe I'll do something different this time. Something that will challenge me.' The more she talked about it, the more tempting it sounded.

'I see. Well, find out if they've got something for me while you're there, will you?'

'Come with me. They might have something that would suit you.' It was an impetuous suggestion and one she instantly regretted. Dan was the last person she wanted with her. He wouldn't be able to stop himself from advising her, interfering and generally being authoritative.

'OK, you're on. We'll call in at my place for me to smarten myself up, Um, are you going like that?' He was indicating her T shirt and jeans.

'No. I'll change too. You go on. I'll pick you up in half-an-hour.'

It was while she was changing that the phone once more rang in the bedroom. Kate nervously regarded it. What if it was the same as last night? Maybe she should ignore it again? Maybe, if she kept ignoring it, whoever it was would give up and stop? Or maybe she should get an answering machine? That way she could monitor every call before picking up on it. Why hadn't she thought of that before? How incredibly stupid of her. But even as she had the thought, her hand was reaching for the receiver.

'H-hello.' She wouldn't be able to bear it if there was no-one there.

'Kate?'

'Oh, Fergal.' She didn't know if the fact that it was Fergal made her feel better or worse. After the way he'd treated her last time, and the manner in which he'd flirted with Sally.

'How are you?'

He sounded a tad hesitant; just as he had when he'd invited her to the ball. Maybe he wasn't as self-confident as he always seemed? Maybe he had fears and insecurities the same as everyone else did?

'I'm fine. Um, you didn't ring me last night, did you?' she blurted.

'No? Why do you ask?'

'It was another of those silent phone calls, and I just wondered,' she went on lamely. Oh no! Why had she mentioned it? Of course, it wouldn't have been Fergal. He would have spoken.

As if he'd read her thoughts, he asked, 'Why on earth would I phone you and not speak? Hang on, are you suggesting it was me making the other calls?' The hesitancy had vanished at a stroke. Now, he just sounded furious; outraged, in fact.

'N-no, of course not. I-I just wondered . . . ' She swallowed. This was the second time she'd implied that he could be her persecutor. He'd never forgive her now — not unless she could come up with a very good reason for her question. 'Um . . . ' inspiration struck, 'as you'd said we needed to talk, you remember, the evening you took Sally and I out? Well, I wondered if perhaps it was you and you couldn't get a connection — you know, on your mobile.'

'Oh, I see.' He sounded slightly less miffed. 'Well, no, it wasn't me. Did you dial 1471 afterwards?'

'Yes. No joy though.'

'If you're worried, you should tell the police.'

'Yes, maybe I will.'

'OK. Well, as I said we need to talk. Get things clear between us.'

Kate put the phone down. She'd agreed to meet him that evening. If only he knew what he was in for. Because crunch time had arrived.

She was determined to find the courage to tell him the truth. Then she'd tell Irene. It was time to come clean.

If she and Fergal were to have any sort of future together, providing, of course, that that was what he wanted to talk about, she had to tell him the truth. Of course, that could mean that things came to a crashing halt between them but she'd have to take that chance.

She couldn't go on as she was, deceiving everyone, lying. And after she'd done that she'd go to the police and tell them what was happening. Whoever was behind the campaign of terror had to be stopped. And maybe they would be if they knew the police were actively involved?

★ ★ ★

When she got to Dan's house and rang the bell, there was no answer. Had he changed his mind about going to the job centre? She was tempted to simply carry on and leave him, but her conscience got the better of her, as it invariably did, and she banged on the door with her hand.

From somewhere at the top of the house, she dimly heard, 'Come in. Door's open. I'll only be five minutes.'

She wandered in, through a square hallway. It was the first time she'd been in — amazingly. But then, there'd been no need, Dan had always come to hers. She looked around.

The house was much bigger than it looked from the outside. The hall alone was as large as her sitting room. A curving staircase swept upwards, to split at the top into two. Crikey! How many bedrooms were there?

Its upkeep must need a substantial amount of money. More than Dan had at present, she would have thought. So, how was he managing?

She went through the first of the doors leading off the hall and found herself in a palatial dining room. She was about to walk out again and go in search of the sitting room when the sight of floor to ceiling bookshelves distracted her.

As Fergal had already discovered, one of Kate's greatest loves was books — of any kind: fiction, contemporary and historical; biographies; autobiographies. She'd often thought she should work in a book shop. Now, there was a thought. There wasn't a decent book shop in Great Mindon, other than a second hand one. Maybe she should open one, specialise in more literary fiction. Her heartbeat quickened.

She walked across to the shelves and reached out for a biography of Daphne du Maurier. As she did so, something else caught her eye. It looked like a child's scrapbook.

She pulled it out; it was a scrapbook. She opened it. It was full of newspaper clippings. All about wealthy, successful women. One in particular caught her attention.

It was a report about someone called Elizabeth Corbett. Now where had she heard that name before? There was a photograph. She was exceptionally beautiful. That was it! Fergal had mentioned her.

She was the woman Dan had been harassing — according to Fergal, that was. Kate's eye skimmed the details. Her husband, an immensely wealthy financier, had died and she'd been his sole beneficiary. He'd completely excluded his two children from a former marriage from his will. They were seeking to have it overturned. She turned the page and something fluttered to the floor.

Another newspaper cutting. She bent to pick it up and saw her own face staring up at her from beneath the headline: *She staked a pound and got 11 million back!*

Kate stopped breathing.

'Kate? Where are you?' Dan poked his head around the door that she'd left open behind her. She didn't have to see his expression as his glance took in the sight of her with the scrap book to know who her tormentor was.

'It's been you — all the time!' She began to shake. 'How could you? How could you, Dan? Pretending to be my friend. Offering to come round whenever.'

He crossed to her and snatched the piece of paper and the scrapbook from her. 'It's not what you think.'

'Oh no? So you don't make a practice of tormenting rich women?'

'What do you mean?'

'Fergal told me about your pursuit of this — Elizabeth Corbett.'

'Fergal should mind his own business.'

'Did you try and scare her? Stalk her? Watch her? Make silent phone calls? It was all you, wasn't it?'

Dan didn't respond. His skin had paled.

She snorted. 'Nothing to say? That's not like you, Dan. You're usually only too ready with your advice. Your warnings. Bit of luck my moving next door, wasn't it? Well, a miracle, in fact. How long did it take you to recognise me?'

'About two seconds,' he snapped. The colour had returned to his face. In fact, it was almost puce now.

'Why didn't you say something?'

'I don't know. But then, when you didn't say anything,' he shrugged, 'I decided to play along with you. I soon realised you weren't going to mention it. It's really not what you think, Kate.'

'So you've just said. It's not the fact that you're out of work and broke, and I'm a lottery winner then? That's got nothing to do with it? I don't understand, Dan. Perhaps you'd like to explain. Why terrorise me? Why simply ask me for some money if you needed it? I would have given it to you.'

'Because it wasn't just the money.' He burst out. He noted Kate's expression. It was one of deep scepticism. He started to backtrack. 'Well, initially it was, I'll be honest.'

Kate snorted with contempt. 'That'll be a first, then.'

'But that didn't last long. I soon realised it was you I wanted, the money was just an added bonus. You must have seen my interest, that I was falling for you? But you . . . ' he stabbed a finger at her, 'you didn't want to know, did you? Not really; not in the way I wanted. It was always Fergal — hanging around in the background. Unwanted, unneeded.'

Kate was tempted to retort, 'Speak for yourself', but decided that might be unwise.

She was alone here with him, after all. For the first time then, the perils of her situation occurred to her. Was she in danger? Would Dan hurt her? He'd shown signs of violence once or twice.

Her heart began to thunder against her ribs, almost painfully so. She had to get out.

Dan's tone had become one of accusation now. 'So, I came up with a plan. I thought if I scared you, just a little — '

'Just a little?' she cried. 'You terrified me — that's not showing an interest or falling in love!'

He ignored her outburst. 'I wanted you to turn to me. I thought you'd fall in love with me — we'd fall in love.' He was beginning to look angry now, as if the whole thing was in some way her fault. Kate very, very slowly took a step backwards — away from him. 'I do love you, Kate; honestly.'

'So, tell me, Dan, would you still want me if I was poor?'

He didn't answer.

'Clearly not. And I notice you first said that I would fall in love with you, you loving me was very much of an afterthought, wasn't it? Well, I can tell you now, Dan, you've been wasting your time, because there's very little left of the eleven million.'

'What?' His colour deepened even more as his anger intensified. Kate took another step away from him. 'You've spent it! All of it? What on, for goodness sake?'

He made no attempt to hide his sheer frustration that such immense wealth was gone. Kate felt a shaft of real fear now. It sliced into her, almost paralysing in its intensity. No-one knew she was here; no-one would hear any call for help that she might be driven to make.

Desperately, she sought to calm him. 'I gave most of it away — to various charities, trusts. So, you see, I'm no good to you any more.'

She tried to walk past him, out of the room. She just wanted to get away from this man who was beginning to look increasingly unhinged.

He stopped her by laying a hand on her arm. 'Don't tell me you're carrying on with this charade of visiting the job centre?' He snorted with bitter amusement.

Kate swung her head to stare at him. How could she ever have thought him attractive? Been attracted to him? His eyes had narrowed, his lips tightened into mean lines. He looked like a different man.

'I'm going, Dan, and I'd be grateful if you'd stay away from me from now on.' Her voice shook uncontrollably.

'Are you going to tell the police?'

'No, as long as you don't bother me any more and don't tell anyone about my win. I want to be the one to tell people. I've been driven from one home, I don't intend to be driven from another.'

'Kate, just before you go — '

She looked at him.

'How much money did you keep?'

Overt curiosity and something else blazed from his face. He couldn't resist speculating — hoping, even now, she realised. 'That's none of your business, Dan. Goodbye.'

And this time, he let her go.

Kate Confesses All

That evening, Kate prepared to go and meet Fergal, her mind still reeling at what Dan had confessed to, that and the sheer, mind-numbing fear she'd felt in his presence towards the end. Yet, if she were honest, her main emotion, now that it was over, was one of relief.

Relief that she could be absolutely, one hundred per cent sure, that it wasn't Fergal behind the incidents. Because, for all her feelings for him, she hadn't been able to rid herself of that last, niggling little doubt. Now, all she had to do was find the right words, as well as the courage, to tell him the truth, and hope he wouldn't be so disgusted with her deception that he simply walked away from her.

They'd arranged to meet in The Red Lion at eight o'clock. She arrived just after eight to find Fergal already there.

He got to his feet as she walked over to him.

'Hello, Kate. Thanks for coming.'

'That's OK. You were right. We do need to talk.'

'A glass of wine?' he asked, picking up the bottle that was on the table in front of him.

Kate nodded, glancing around the bar as she did so. Apart from a couple of occupied tables on the other side of the room, they were alone. She didn't know whether that made the situation better or worse. If there were more people around Fergal might be loath to make a scene. 'Cheers.' She raised her glass to, her mouth with a hand that shook.

'Fergal.'

'Kate.'

They spoke simultaneously. Fergal smiled. 'Sorry, you first.'

'No, please, you asked to meet so you go first.'

'Kate,' Fergal reached across the table and covered one of her hands with both of his, 'you must realise how I'm beginning to feel about you. That I'm falling in love with you. I made the mistake of trying to rush things, against my better judgement, but I've wanted to hold you so badly, right from the first time I saw you, in fact.'

'Me too.'

Fergal made no attempt to hide his surprise at that. His fingers tightened over hers. Kate felt the by now familiar jolt of emotion. 'But then why didn't you say something?' he asked.

'It's a long story, but if you're prepared to listen, I'll tell you.'

So she did just that. He knew most of it, but she went through it all once more. She told him how, at times, she'd suspected anyone that she'd ever known, including him, briefly.

He nodded at this point. 'Yes, I did get that message.'

'I'm sorry.' She went on to tell him that that day she'd discovered that Dan was the one behind it all.

'Dan Peters?' He snorted contemptuously. 'Can't say I'm surprised, after the way he harassed that other poor woman, Elizabeth Corbett I think her name was. I believe I mentioned his name in connection with the intruder in your garden. But why on earth would he do such things? How did you find out it was him?'

'He kept a scrapbook, full of newspaper cuttings. This morning I called to pick him up — we were going to the job centre together. While I was waiting for him I saw it. I'd been browsing through his shelves of books and when I opened the scrapbook, a newspaper cutting fell out.'

Fergal frowned. 'Perhaps I'm being stupid but I don't quite see — '

'The cutting was about me.'

'You? Are you someone famous and I haven't recognised you?' He was frowning by this time, his hand still upon hers.

'Well, you could say that, I suppose.'

'Kate, you'll have to stop talking in riddles!'

'I came into possession of some money. Quite a lot of money.'

'Yes. You told me, about your parents dying.'

'No, that's not the money I'm talking about.'

Fergal didn't move a muscle as he waited for her to continue. She saw a spasm of fear flash into his face, then it was gone again.

'I won the lottery. It's a wonder, actually, that everyone here didn't know — you included.' He stared at her in silence. 'It was in the papers, national and local — a friend — Sally, actually — talked out of turn. They managed to photograph me leaving my flat. That's the photo that Dan had.'

'Ye-es. I do vaguely recall seeing something. I didn't take much notice.'

'It was rather a large win. Sally persuaded me to buy the ticket. I wasn't in the habit of doing so.'

He removed his hand from hers. Kate felt a sinking in the pit of her stomach. Just as she'd feared, he despised her.

'Dan felt I should — share my good fortune.'

'So how would scaring you half to death achieve that.'

'He said he thought I would turn to him for protection, fall in love with him, then — '

'Oh, I get it. You'd marry your saviour and your good fortune would be his good fortune.'

'Yes.'

'Well, I'm relieved that I'm not still under suspicion.' He leant back in his seat, his one hand toying with the stem of his glass, his eyes twin slits in a face that was completely devoid of expression.

Kate said nothing to this. What could she say, after all? 'Tell me, I'm curious, if I was a suspect, why did you agree to come out with me?'

'Well, I suppose, deep down, I knew it wasn't you. You see — ' she ploughed on, 'initially, I couldn't see what the motive was. There was no demand for money, no threat. Apart from the anonymous letters, the first of which promised to keep my secret — for now, and the second which said he'd be watching me. Anyway, after a while, I began to expect a demand for money, to put an end to it.' Miserably, she limped into silence.

'I see.' His expression still provided no clue as to his feelings about what she'd just told him. 'So, tell me, how big was this win of yours?'

'Eleven million.'

'My word!' Fergal's face blanched.

'Quite! That's why I didn't tell anyone — it had already caused so much resentment and jealousy. I thought the same thing might happen here. Even Sally changed towards me. We ended up not speaking.' Her voice broke at the memory. 'That's why I had to move. To get away from it all. It's also why I halted things between us. I felt I couldn't let you go on wooing me while I wasn't being totally honest. Even if I hadn't discovered it was Dan behind everything, I was going to tell you, and Irene, the truth and take my chances. I couldn't go on living a lie.'

She stumbled to a halt. 'I'm sorry.'

Fergal didn't speak, although she would have sworn she saw a momentary softening of his face. Kate could see how his mind was working though. Her news had put a whole new slant upon what he'd been going to say to her; she could see that as clearly as if he'd spoken the words out loud. He was going to walk away from her, no matter what his feelings were for her. No way was Fergal Cameron going to be labelled a fortune hunter, placed in the same category as Dan.

'Of course, what Dan didn't know,' Kate spoke slowly, for maximum effect, 'was that I've given most of it away.'

She watched as the colour gradually seeped back into Fergal's face. He opened his mouth to say something, but then obviously thought better of it and closed it again.

'I kept just enough to make my life reasonably comfortable and maybe start a business of my own. I suppose I should have told everyone that from the first, but I didn't know what to do. As I said, after what happened before, you know, once bitten and all that, but it was wrong to deceive everyone.'

Fergal's face showed the first glimmering of understanding.

'Anyway, I gave almost all of it to charity. I've given some to Sally and I plan to invest most of the rest of it for any children I might be fortunate enough to have. I am going to keep enough back to buy myself a small book shop and stock it. But what it all means is that I intend to work for my living the same as anyone else. And it also means that any man who might be interested in me — for myself alone — need never feel he'll be accused of loving me for my money.' She couldn't help smiling at this point. Fergal was looking positively stunned. 'Of course, if he's really upset by all of this, I could give the rest of it away as well. I'm truly sorry, Fergal, but, as I said, deep in my heart, I always knew it wasn't you.'

'There's no need to give any more

money away, Kate. I think you've done more than enough and I can assure you we're operating from a more or less even playing field. Of course, if you'd still been in possession of that eleven million, I might have been struggling to match you, for a while at any rate.' He shrugged.

Kate frowned at him. 'But I-I thought you said — '

'What? What did I say?'

'Well, the evening of the ball, you said you could do with a bit more money.'

He nodded. 'It's true, there have been times when I would have been glad of some extra money. After buying that last garage, life was a little difficult, cash flow problems, mainly. But I've recovered from that. These past few months have been very good for me. So much so, that I'm considering buying another. And this time, in case you're wondering, I can easily afford to.

'I'm so glad we've got that sorted out.'

She was giddily and deliriously happy all of a sudden.

Fergal led her into his house where he'd arranged Irene to be waiting. 'I knew you'd want your good friend here, maybe you'd like to tell her all about the past few weeks?'

So she did, and her good friend simply hugged her. Words were unnecessary.

Without any more ado, Fergal took Kate into his arms. 'I'm in love with you. That hasn't changed. I want you, with or without money. I hope you feel the same about me.'

'I do.'

His eyes gleamed from beneath heavy lids. 'Are those two little words a promise of things to come?'

Thoroughly disconcerted by his murmured question, Kate felt herself blushing.

'Have you become very attached to that cottage? Or would you consider eventually leaving it when we marry?'

Kate felt a shaft of pure joy then. So

much so that her voice trembled as she said, 'If someone made me the right offer.'

'And how would Jess feel about a move, do you think?'

'Jess will be happy to be wherever I am.'

'Splendid.'

Kate began to chuckle. 'You've got it all worked out, haven't you?'

'Oh yes, and have had for quite some time. I just needed to convince the love of my life to feel the same way about me as I do about her. Have I succeeded, do you think?'

For an answer, Kate lifted her face to his once more.

THE END

We do hope that you have enjoyed reading this large print book.

Did you know that all of our titles are available for purchase?

We publish a wide range of high quality large print books including:
**Romances, Mysteries, Classics
General Fiction
Non Fiction and Westerns**

Special interest titles available in large print are:
**The Little Oxford Dictionary
Music Book, Song Book
Hymn Book, Service Book**

Also available from us courtesy of Oxford University Press:
**Young Readers' Dictionary
(large print edition)
Young Readers' Thesaurus
(large print edition)**

For further information or a free brochure, please contact us at:
**Ulverscroft Large Print Books Ltd.,
The Green, Bradgate Road, Anstey,
Leicester, LE7 7FU, England.
Tel:** (00 44) **0116 236 4325
Fax:** (00 44) **0116 234 0205**

Other titles in the
Linford Romance Library:

AS TIME GOES BY

Gillian Villiers

When Lally caretakes her grandmother's croft in the wildest part of Scotland, she fully expects that she'll return soon, to a high-powered job in Edinburgh. Her scatterbrained sister Bel has other plans though, and Lally quickly finds the people and the place seeping into her soul. Or is it just one person, in the shape of new neighbour Iain? Torn between two worlds, Lally's decision will not only impact on herself, but also on everyone else around her.

A CERTAIN SMILE

Beth James

Freya has been made redundant and her high-flying boyfriend, Jay, is pressurising her to join him in London. But this would mean her leaving the place her heart lies — her home in the New Forest. And there are so many things to consider: her friends, her small cottage and her adorable, little dog Henri . . . and there's a certain dog walker with good legs and a friendly smile. Freya knows that she'd miss saying 'good morning' to him too.